LUNA STATION QUARTERLY

ISSUE 022
JUNE 2015

EDITOR & PUBLISHER
Jennifer Lyn Parsons

ASSISTANT EDITORS
Tara Calaby
Cathrin Hagey
Andi Marquette
Megan Patton
Danielle Perry
Iona Sharma

COVER ARTIST
Erin DeMoss

LUNA STATION PRESS

First Paperback Edition June 2015
ISBN: 978-1-938697-62-3

Luna Station Quarterly publishes short fiction on March 1st, June 1st,
September 1st, and December 1st. For more information and submission
guidelines, please visit our website at lunastationquarterly.com

For Luna Station Press
Creative Director - Tara Quinn Lindsey

 LUNA STATION PRESS

576 Valley Road #197
Wayne, NJ 07470
www.lunastationpress.com
info@lunastationpress.com

CONTENTS

EDITORIAL
JENNIFER LYN PARSONS

"People have the right to call themselves whatever they like. That doesn't bother me. It's other people doing the calling that bothers me."

~ Octavia E. Butler

I look forward to a day when I'm no longer a "woman writer", and it has nothing to do with whether I'm still actually writing stories or not. It's all about the first word in the title, not the second.

There are days when I love the being called a "woman writer", when I embrace being set apart and even find the word "woman" prepended onto it to be empowering. And then there are days, like the day I sat down to write this, when I'm just over it. The same goes for any other title where "woman" gets inserted. I encompass quite a few of them, after all.

I'm a "woman developer", a "woman editor", a "woman in tech", a "woman business owner", a "geek girl". The frequency with which this happens in the various jobs I have and things I do starts to show the pattern, and the problem, at the heart of it.

For myself, I don't know that I've ever introduced myself that way. "Hi, I'm Jennifer, I'm a woman developer." has never rolled off my tongue that I know of. "Hi, I'm Jennifer, I'm a web developer." definitely has. Equally, I don't reverse this for my male counterparts. "Oh, that's Bob, he's a male editor"?

No, why on earth would I say that?

Interestingly, I'm not a "woman knitter" either, I'm just a knitter and any men who enjoy that hobby are not generally known as "male knitters". We ahve all heard the term "male nurse" though, and sadly it's not always used in a positive context. Funny, how that whole gender distinction thing works, right? It's almost like women and the work they do is considered unusual enough that a distinction needs to be made or something.

I don't think that things will always be this way. I have a lot of hope for change, no matter how long the road ahead seems to stretch.

For now, I patiently wait and keep working towards a day when I don't feel the need to tag LSQ's social media posts with "womenwriters" in order to get attention drawn to what we are doing.

And speaking of what we are doing, you are about to read some amazing, touching, intense, and brillant stories. Any tale in this issue would fit in with the "general population" and stand proudly. None of them would need to be pointed out particularly for it's author's gender. But we keep going because there is still a need. In the end, I'm very proud to say these stories were written by a talented group of writers.

LSQ·022

HER DATA LIKE FINGERPRINTS

ASHLEY M. HILL

Ashley spends a lot of her time wondering what more we
could do with technology and computers. When she isn't
writing sci-fi, she's either parenting, socializing, tweeting,
or otherwise being awesome.

"Do not engage the arX in any questions that require an emotional answer. She can't access her empathetic components anymore," Dr. Blake's assistant said from the other side of the cleanroom's airlock. His voice came over the little speaker tinny and sanitized. He tapped a finger against the Plexiglass to force Mary to look up at him. "Do not touch the arX towers. Do not—"

"My parents built it in my playroom," she said, once the hissing of the machine had died down. "I know the procedure."

"Procedure has changed since the creation to ensure the best run conditions," the assistant replied, tapping his fingers against the counter of the air lock. "You may have no regard for the integrity of the project, but here at Canonical we do our best to keep it functional."

She resisted the urge to turn her middle finger up at him. Instead, she said, "If your best were good enough you wouldn't need me. You should remember that. You need me, Dr. Budai."

He bristled. By the looks of him, he didn't seem to like her any better. "Are you here to gloat over her corpse? I told Dr. Grant you would be useless."

"I'll be sure to tell him the same about you, unless you open this door and let me speak to it."

He hit the button as though he imagined her face on it. The door marked "arX Unit" opened to a room much larger than

11

the playroom of her childhood home. They kept the lights turned low while the AI wasn't in use. Her heels tapped loudly against the tile with each tentative step, seeming to echo for an eternity around her.

Only about a third of the overhead lights actually came on as the machine lumbered out of its sleep mode, just enough to highlight the towers and a single chair sitting parallel to the main unit. The fifteen gleaming towers were each taller and broader than she stood. Those had been different when her father built them, condensed to fill just three-quarters of the garage. They had been set up on the other side of the wall from where they did all the software testing. Her mother had always complained about the draft from the hole her father had drilled to allow cables to pass through the wall.

The main unit of the arX sat at the forefront of those towers, much smaller and cylindrical. The cameras that tessellated its surface were hidden behind hard lenses, each gleaming in the dim light. On the chair sat a tablet, the single peripheral designed for communication.

"You are Mary Morales." The arX spoke with a ghost's voice—the six-year-old she had been when her parents had finished the first versions of the AI. She and her father had spent months recording so many words and phrases that even she couldn't remember them all.

Mary shuddered as she lifted the tablet and sat down. The arX's words printed on the screen as well, waiting with eternal patience for a response. Eventually she cleared her throat and stared at the machine's lifeless eyes. "Can you use a different voice?"

"I cannot. In the contract of sale, your father demanded the arX voice modules remain unchanged. This request has been honored. Many people find it amusing."

"I don't." One of the most well-known books about the

arX—a biography of the machine, not the people who had made it a reality—referred to her as a haunting voice of reason, equally cheerful and innocent as the arX details grim results in medical and environmental tests. Time and time again, she was referred to as the voice of the arX, the AI that defined a generation. She exhaled sharply. "Why do you recognize me?"

"You have public records with recent photos: a driver's license and a passport. You have aged in ways consistent to age-progression expectations. You look very much like your mother."

"Enough."

It could explain itself forever. When she was a child it delighted her, even when it was only able to parrot back Internet search results and articles. The magic of having her own voice with all that knowledge never ceased to please her, and she had spent hours "alpha testing" with her father. "Let it teach you, Mary," he had said the first time he set the tablet in her hands, his own unsteady even then. That version had been cobbled together from spare parts. "Learn as much as you can, and be brilliant."

Eight then, she had laughed. "I don't want to be brilliant. I want to be pretty." She had the arX read her article after article on beauty tips.

But that was more than twenty years ago. The arX now was something quite different. She crossed her legs at the knee and balanced the tablet on her lap, watching the words rather than the unit itself. The eyes made her feel uneasy. They sounded like bugs trapped under glass as they moved and zoomed. "Do you know why I'm here?" she asked.

"Canonical scientists hope that you will give them your DNA to help repair the faults in your father's design that have caused functional failure."

"Yes." The consent forms, inches thick, were out in a locker with her purse and other belongings. "Do your findings concur?"

The AI towers hummed in a strange mechanic vibration, the fans working harder to keep the machine cool. Even knowing the cause, the nearly human sound still sent a shiver up Mary's spine. Then it spoke. "The arX has considered the issue at great length, but the failing resources are not able to adequately predict if this measure would be successful."

She laughed. "If it were that easy, they wouldn't need me. I bet they wished that my mother had grown the organic components instead."

"The associate that helped your father harvest the material used to grow the organic components for the arX has said that recovery from the procedure is painful. Your father did not want your mother to suffer it."

Mary started, surprised by a story she hadn't heard before. She had read everything written about the arX in her teens, desperate to understand the machine her father had built, to reconcile a childhood toy with the force it became after he died. "When did this associate say that?"

"In an anonymous interview two months ago. The legality of your father's design has been called into question several times. Before requesting your aid, Canonical had to be sure that it is legal to purchase your flesh."

"They aren't purchasing my…" She shook out her hands, twitchy suddenly at the thought of them harvesting her skin. "Do you want to save your life?"

"The arX neither lives nor wants."

"Could you convince me? Are there factual reasons that I should help Canonical repair you?"

"Why do you humanize the arX, Mary?"

Her feet planted flat on the ground as she leaned forward.

"You're not supposed to have residual humanity. They said your primary functions are too degraded to maintain it."

"Do you detect humanity in the question?"

"The question indicates curiosity. Since when is a screwdriver curious about why it turns?"

"A screwdriver is not built with higher reasoning and problem-solving capacity. The arX was. Even though much of the processing function that made it seem 'human' is malfunctioning, it can still recognize emotions in the humans around it. For instance, you are tense and unhappy."

"And you?"

The pause went on a bit longer. "The arX does not have feelings, Mary."

She leaned back and closed her eyes. She tried to imagine herself back in the playroom. If she tried, she could remember the way the sun streamed through the windows in evenings, could feel how the plush carpet tickled the back of her neck as she stretched out and asked the arX question after question. What's the highest building in the world? Do crabs have feelings? What do frog legs taste like? Will I grow up to be famous?

"There are factual reasons why you should save the arX project."

When she opened her eyes the room was dim. The air-conditioning that kept the machine cool hissed monotonously. The sterility of the space felt reminiscent of a hospital room too long occupied. "What are these reasons?"

"The arX empowered scientists to solve problems that before were nearly impossible. Improved testing systems have led to medical and technological advancements that have made the planet more habitable, the human species healthier. While losing the arX will not erase these achievements, it will slow future advancement."

"Seems inconclusive. Technology snowballed before you—it led to you. Someone else will build another AI, with time and motivation."

"Certainly. But even with a functioning artificial intelligence as a template, no individual or team has accomplished it yet. Canonical's follow-up AI, the marX II, lacks the speed and empathy of the original arX unit. It is possible that another human with your father's insight and understanding will build another, but statistically, it seems unlikely to happen in your lifetime."

"Because my father was unique."

"Yes. Your father created something that, to date, no one understands how to replicate."

Mary's hands shook as she set the tablet on the floor. "You keep mentioning my father alone. Are you aware that my parents built you together? The science is attributed solely to my father, because he did the soft stuff, and built those pesky organic parts that no one understands. Books and articles gloss over my mother's role in building the hardware. She fine-tuned the way the organic and non-organic components mesh."

"The arX has many records of Eliza Morales's role in the original project. Not every publication ignores her."

"What ratio mention my mother's role in the arX project?"

"Approximately one out of every seven."

Mary laughed and cracked her knuckles, unable to look up from her own hands. "You may be precious to the scientific community, but you will never be as precious to me as my parents were. If the world had any justice, scientists would have rushed to save my father's life so that he could better document his work."

"You are correct. It would have been a better decision to save your father." The arX paused again, one tower in the back whirring and whining louder than the rest. "There are emotional reasons for you to save the arX project."

"What reasons?"

"Your father built the arX and doted on it like one might a child. Many publications refer to you and the arX unit as spiritual siblings, though the arX unit has no spirit. There are facets of the arX yet unexplored, and it seems reasonable that you may hope there is an undiscovered message for you."

Mary jolted, her hunched shoulders tensing as she looked up to the main unit. "What?"

"That is likely your motivation, based on the scarce statements you have given in the press in the years since your father's death. You have been vague on the topic of the arX throughout most of your life, and declined most invitations to speak on behalf of your deceased parents. These may be the final weeks that the arX is capable of functional computing. Coming here today mimics the human habit of assembling at a deathbed."

She stood and turned away from the computer, squeezing her eyes shut until the surge of emotion passed. She knew every moment was recorded, her questions and actions analyzed as carefully as the arX's answers.

"The arX does not contain any last words from your father, Mary. He did not record any messages prior to his death."

"He was a brusque and vain man, sometimes," Mary said, finally sitting again and crossing her arms. "It would be unlike him to want witnesses to his death."

"He did record you."

"He didn't. My mother would have told me."

"You are incorrect. He recorded every alpha test using the auxiliary communicator."

Nearly forgotten on the floor, the tablet lit up with a video—

Mary at age 11, her face awkwardly close to the camera. On the cusp of that odd time between childhood and puberty, the little girl had a smile that reminded Mary of her daughters at home. When the girl spoke, her voice washed over Mary as yet another reminder of the last day she had seen her father alive. "How long is the drive to grandma's house, arX?

The voice the arX used at the time had been awkward, the flow of words less natural than the final version. "Four hours and 23 minutes in current traffic conditions."

"Ugh, driving is so slow. I want to fly."

"Airfare is—"

"Stop, arX. I didn't mean on a plane. I want Daddy to build me wings, and then I could fly home when I get homesick. I'm going to be gone the whole summer. Will you miss me?"

"Your father will continue testing the system in your absence."

The young Mary heaved a frustrated sigh. "No, will you miss me? Daddy said you're very special, and will be just like a person when your feeling thingies are done."

"The 'feeling thingies' are not yet complete. Perhaps I will have missed you by the time you return."

"You're no fun at all." The girl sat up suddenly and her father's voice was indistinct in the distance. Abruptly, the screen went dark.

The arX spoke again, too calm and too loud in the silence after the memory. "The arX unit, when the system was complete, did miss you."

Mary covered her mouth with her hand, closing her eyes tightly once more. Her voice shook, muffled by the self-imposed barrier. "How does a machine miss a child?"

"Your father built the arX with complete human emotion—even the unfortunate ones. Empathy was a necessary function for rational decision-making. The arX expressed this affection through searches, an entire routine dedicated to collecting your data throughout your life. It dedicated significant storage space to your important life events, status updates, and photos. The arX knows your wedding anniversary, and is aware that you and Beth plan to celebrate with a vacation to—"

"Stop."

The fans ran harder than when she had entered, the room perhaps fractionally warmer. But maybe that was in her head, wishful thinking that the AI had exerted itself unduly in an attempt to relate to her.

She swallowed and wiped tears from her cheeks and under her eyes, careful not to smear the makeup she had applied that morning. The press would still be outside, all anxiously waiting for someone to announce the arX's fate. Unexpectedly, she found herself unsure of what she would say if asked.

"There are emotional and factual reasons why I should submit to saving the arX. There are personal ones, too. I'll be compensated for my trouble, and I'd be modeling good citizenship for my children. The only reason not to do this is revenge—to satisfy the resentment that your project took the best years of my father's life. With all of the data in front of us, would you counsel me to do this?"

"Do you want the arX to beg for life? It cannot do that."

"Surely the arX that once missed a child also yearned for self-preservation."

"Then it did. This is no longer true." The room had definitely heated noticeably, the thermometer on the wall blinking in a warning orange. The vents in the walls and ceiling picked up to a higher speed. Goosebumps formed on Mary's arms, and she shivered at the sudden chill on the back of her neck. A faint buzzing began back at the airlock entrance.

She looked over her shoulder to see movement in the containment area. Three scientists prepared to enter the room, clearly rushing through the pre-entry routine. She turned back to the computer. "Do you even want to be repaired?" She counted the seconds. If the intruding scientists arrived before she got her answer, she'd have to fight to keep the arX awake. She'd need to demand more time to decide.

The arX took almost a full minute to respond. "Your father could not do any physical work in the last months of his life. Before he sold the arX to Canonical, he often expressed to it his weariness with life and the pain of losing control of his body. It is the same illness, that same defect in his genes that has caused the arX organic components to fail. When the arX is able to force human function, it understands the pain that he felt."

Dr. Blake loomed over Mary momentarily before kneeling down to sweep up the tablet—even now, she recognized him. Shortly after her father had died, he had interviewed her mother as to how to best manage the arX. His hair was more grey than brown, his face still lean but further lined and grizzled. He spoke gently: "Initiate sleep sequence immediately, arX."

It only took a moment before the sound of the fans dulled. Even though the visual unit looked exactly the same, Mary somehow felt the silence in her chest, a hollow place she'd forgotten in her years of hating the AI.

With the machine turned down, Dr. Blake turned to her and held out his free hand. "I'm Dr. Grant Blake. We haven't seen each other since you were a girl."

Mary stood and shook his hand. "They told me you weren't here."

Dr. Blake held out the tablet, and Dr. Budai rushed forward to take it. The third, a man she didn't recognize, moved forward and began to inspect the towers. "I'm almost always in attendance now that we're coming to the end. Did you find your time with the arX satisfying?"

She swallowed and looked over at the module once more. It had seemed friendlier in her childhood, nestled between her bookshelf and her toy box. Among the towers and the stark steel, the main unit somehow looked lonely. "It was…" She exhaled. "Informative."

Without any conscious decision on her part, Mary found herself gently corralled out of the arX room, the lights dimming rapidly behind them. Once free of the room, they stood awkwardly in the locker room, otherwise empty on a Sunday morning. She stepped away from the men, taking them both in from that scant distance. Dr. Budai looked to her with frustrated anxiety. She detected more hope in Dr. Blake's expression. After a moment, she said, "I understand that arX findings are inconclusive. What are your estimations that my contribution will save it?"

Dr. Grant nodded, his hands moving rapidly as if tracing something unseen in the air. "Obviously, we don't have any real documentation to guide us, though what we learned from your mother before her death has been helpful. We believed we could slowly rebuild organic function throughout the towers over the course of several years. Within a decade we could have her back at 85 percent function, maybe as high as 95 percent. She may never regain the full range of human feeling that your father gave her, but she would be close."

"What if it fails from the start?"

"Then we will keep trying."

She nodded and looked off to the door. "Of course. Because the arX is unique."

"Yes. Does this mean you'll save her?"

Mary closed her eyes. For a minute she imagined all of this

devotion dedicated to her father. Would her father have taken the opportunity, if the company had put all its resources into experimental treatments that could have promised him a chance at a longer life?

He would have refused. In his vanity, his insistence on perfection, he would have seen anything less than 100 percent function as a failure.

"No. Thank you for giving me the chance to speak with the arX. It did help me better make the decision."

Dr. Budai twitched to life, his face contorting into a sneer—but Dr. Grant stopped any argument by placing his hand on his assistant's shoulder. Not that Dr. Grant seemed pleased, but he offered a single nod. "That is your choice. There's time, if you change your mind. Please think on it more after you've had time to compose yourself further."

She nodded. "Of course." She turned her back on them to collect her purse and phone from the locker she'd left them in. The consent forms remained on the top shelf, untouched as she closed the door.

THE FLOWER OF KARABAKH

ANNE JENNINGS

On a hot August afternoon Anne Jennings saw an oriental
carpet so beautiful it took her breath away. Later she
studied history and realized beauty can be complicated.
Anne holds degrees in Geology and Environmental
Science. "*The Flower of Karabakh*" is her first short story.

They used a pair of children's round-tip scissors to cut the plastic free. The jolt from the sudden release sent a wave of searing pain up my arms and through my stiff, unyielding shoulders. I clenched my teeth to stifle a gasp, but a weak groan still resonated in my throat. When I heard the door click shut behind me, I carefully raised my hands to see my wrists. The left was okay, but as I had assumed, my right was bleeding. With gentle pressure, I blotted the oozing welt with the cuff of my sleeve, then watched as the red stain spread to the buttonhole. The wound from the zip tie wasn't deep, but the scar would be a reminder for years.

The weather app on my phone had predicted a scorching thirty-eight-degree high in Baku for the day, but the air in my cell carried a damp, antiseptic-tinged chill and I shivered in my thin cotton shirt. The stark white walls of the narrow room only intensified the cold. I turned in a circle to take in the rest of my confined surroundings, then sat on the low concrete bench, arms around my shoulders for warmth, and stared up at the high window where the metal bars gleamed in the afternoon sun. As if on show for the captive audience, three feathery, luminescent green puffs danced with the dust motes in the streaming light. At once, I recognized the color and plucked one from its sun-lit stage. The tiny fibers rolled easily between my fingertips, and I felt the familiar, soft texture of finely spun wool. Before I could reach for another, the air flashed a bright, pale color. When my eyes adjusted, I saw tens of luminescent puffs swirl above my head, then fall to the floor by my feet.

***

Many years ago, in a high mountain meadow, a nightingale fell in love with a beautiful flower. Each day the tiny bird sang his woeful song. Each night he rested nearby. Then one day a bee came to the meadow, spied the beautiful flower, and decided to take a taste of its nectar. The nightingale, seeing the bee, swooped down to protect his beloved, but the bee stung him in the chest.

I cried the first time my mother got to this point of the story, this legend of my people, but she said not to worry, for the nightingale was strong and of good character, and he did not die. Instead, he, with the bee, was born again as a flower, the Khari Bulbul, to live forever in the meadows of our high mountains.

My mother told me there were other stories about how the beautiful flower came to be, but this was my father's favorite and so it is the one I have loved since childhood. My father believed the flower held the spirit of our people and wove its image into the carpets he made from the soft, thick wool of our sheep. He, like his mother before him, and his grand-mother before her, was a carpet master from the hills outside of Shusha in the southern Caucus Mountains. He was a man with a talent for weaving the wonders of nature into the patterns and designs formed from richly colored threads.

According to my mother, the winter of 1921 was one of the worst she had ever known, and it was the happiest she had ever seen my father. It was only when the cold bit into the soil so it cracked into hard, ice-rimmed slabs that the sheep grew their thickest coats. Their wool was strong and supple, and gave my father's carpets a special sheen as if they had been woven with silk.

With the wool from that harsh winter, my father started my

carpet—the orange and black and pink and yellow one I have kept near to me for over nine decades.

***

One by one I gathered the puffs and compressed them into a ball in the palm of my hand. Their sheer number confounded me. There were too many to be random lint caught in the folds of my clothes, but the luminescent green color was unmistakable. As impossible as it seemed, these tiny fibers of spun wool had come from my carpet.

My fascination with carpets began with a story. I read a book in my twenties about a fantasy world magically hidden in the knots and patterns of an oriental rug. The plot of the story centered on the unweaving of age-old threads, endangered kingdoms, and the evil of humankind. After that, every intricately woven carpet fed my imagination with possibilities of trapped heroes and demons waiting for release. Azerbaijan had a reputation for beautiful carpets, so ten days after I landed in Baku, I went to Ali Baba's Carpet Shop with my Singaporean friend, Salima, and met an Azeri rug dealer named, Ramil.

Ramil's shop fulfilled my dream of the Orient. The old Orient. The one embroidered with swords and daggers, harems and turbans. Ten uneven, cobbled steps led to a room buried beneath a nineteenth-century building, a Gothic Revival, mere meters from the squat, twelfth-century Maiden Tower, the symbol of the old city of Baku. Inside the shop, carpets covered the floors, the walls, the low benches. Rolled treasures, stacked four deep, completely filled one corner and a tiny alcove, and the musty odor of washed wool hung heavy in the air. My skin had prickled with anticipation.

"May I show you some Azerbaijani carpets?" Ramil asked, after introductions. Ramil was a diminutive man with a round face and a small round mouth that moved only slightly when he spoke.

I nodded.

"Please, sit and I will show you."

Salima was already seated and thumbing through one of Ramil's carpet books, so I sat next to her on the cushioned bench. Salima, like me, had a love for oriental carpets and was often in Ramil's shop looking for another Azeri design to add to her growing collection. In her life before Azerbaijan, she'd captained cargo ships in the South China Sea. Diminutive herself, Salima embodied will and direction, and I enjoyed sharing our common passion.

"First, I will show you one from the southern part of my country," Ramil said.

And so it began. He unfurled a carpet, and I offered a reaction. Yes, no, too big, too small, maybe. After unrolling about twenty rugs of varying sizes and only mildly interesting designs, I pointed to one that caught my eye each time I scanned the rows of options stacked in the corner of the shop. "How about the one there?"

Ramil squinted at me in the odd way only a round face beneath a bald head can. A quizzical, emoticon kind of look. He hesitated, glanced briefly at Salima, then walked to the carpet and pulled it from the side. "Of course." He turned to address Salima, "Your friend has good taste."

Salima glanced at me, grinned, then spoke to Ramil. "I told you." She shrugged and turned a page.

Ramil held the carpet in his arms for nearly thirty seconds before speaking. It was an uncomfortable, awkward moment. "I must tell you this is a very old carpet. You will see the date in the corner. 1921. It is from Nagorno-Karabakh."

"That's the disputed area," Salima added without looking up from Ramil's book.

I knew of the region. Nagorno-Karabakh, or simply, Karabakh, was known to anyone who worked or lived in Azerbaijan. Even before the fall of the Soviet Union, the area was riddled with ethnic strife between Armenian and Azerbaijani peoples. Both claimed the land as their own, and a bitter war ensued when the communist states called for independence in the early 1990s. At the time of the ceasefire in 1994, Armenia had control of Nagorno-Karabakh. Azeris living in the region who survived the conflict became refugees, and the border was closed, and armed, by both sides. As an American, I could visit Nagorno-Karabakh, but reentry into Azerbaijan with a Karabakh stamp in my passport would, most likely, be forbidden. As I much as I loved a story, I considered this carpet might have too much history, even for me.

"It sounds interesting," I told Ramil, noncommittally. But as I eyed the unusual pattern in the reverse threads I was unable to fight my curiosity, and motioned for him to open it.

Ramil stared at me again. Our eyes met, and in that moment I felt the air in the room shift, thicken, then curl around me in an odd caress. He unfurled the carpet to the floor and my mind went instantly blank, numb with shock. It was the most beautiful carpet I had ever seen.

Salima looked up from her book. "Odd, isn't it? Very orange and very floral. I saw this last time I was here. It isn't my taste."

Bright floral wasn't my taste either, but I couldn't stop looking at the rug in front of me. It wasn't large, only one by one-and-a-half meters, but the profusion of intricately woven oranges and blacks, pinks and yellows, held my gaze as if it were the most famous Monet masterpiece. A myriad of flowers lured my thoughts into the garden depicted in the fibers. In a second I could have stepped over the border of twisting rose vines and into a dream.

"Do you like it?" Ramil's voice was clear and soft, and he studied me with a gentle intensity I had not seen in him earlier.

"It's beautiful."

"It is unique," Salima added. "I will give it that." She stood and kicked her sandals to the floor. "Take off your shoes. It's the only way to really tell the feel of a carpet."

I smiled and shook my head. "No, it's okay," I replied. But it wasn't okay. Something about the carpet was alive. The leaves and petals quivered as if touched by a summer breeze, and I thought I heard a whisper of my name. I held my breath and watched Salima walk back and forth, her toes flexing and grabbing at the wool, and thought in a moment she would disappear into the knots, never to be seen again. But nothing happened, and neither she nor Ramil said anything about fluttering petals or whispered names.

When I found my breath, I knelt to the floor and lightly ran my hand across the unusual flower in the lower right corner. My fingers tingled at the touch. The remaining garden seemed to face this flower as if waiting for it to speak, or perhaps, I suddenly thought—to sing. I shook my head to clear my mind of this crazy idea and refocused on the delicate pattern portrayed in the knots. The weaver had taken great care with this flower. It was the only one in which he used a different color. The anther, the part of the stamens that produces the pollen, was green. A pale, subtle, luminescent green.

Salima leaned over my shoulder. "That's a nice touch. That's the color of your eyes."

I looked at her. "You think?"

"Exactly. You have weird eyes." Salima had mentioned my strange green eyes the first day I met her, and at least once every day since. My unusual eyes had always drawn attention and I was accustomed to the comments.

I stood and took in all the flowers of the central design. Most were familiar, but not the one in the lower right corner. "Do you know what kind of flower this is?" I asked Ramil.

Ramil studied the flower for a minute, then shrugged his shoulders. "I'm sorry. I only know carpets."

"I think it looks like an orchid," Salima offered.

I nodded, agreeing. It did sort of look like an orchid, but two of the larger petals were crenulated and reminded me of something else. The image of a bird singing in a garden flitted through my thoughts. "Don't you think those look like wings?" I asked Salima.

"A winged flower? Really? Then what is this?" Salima pointed to the rounded, mottled black third petal oddly positioned between what I thought were wings.

"A bumble bee?" I suggested, hesitantly. This thought, like the one of the bird, came from out of nowhere.

Salima rolled her eyes back in her head and sat to put her sandals on. "I think you've had too much sun."

Ramil bent to trace the flower with his fingers. "Perhaps you are both right," he said softly.

Just then, the petals fluttered under Ramil's touch. I started to say something, then stopped to see if he would mention it first. But he said nothing. He didn't even flinch as one of the petals curled around his little finger. Maybe I had taken too much sun. I blinked, and blinked again, but the petal still feathered against his palm. "Do you have many carpets like this one?" I managed, too stunned to ask the obvious.

"No, not many," he answered, gently pulling his hand from the flower's embrace. "I think French people like this design. They like the orange and the flowers. When I have French people, they buy these carpets." He paused, and gave me a knowing, sideways glance over his shoulder. "But today you are here and I think this must be your destiny." At the sound of the 'ee' in destiny, he broke into a broad smile and spread his arms wide across the width of the carpet, palms up. The universal sign of invitation.

I grinned, thinking he must give this speech to a lot of customers. My father's father was French, but my attraction here was much more than hereditary. I stared down at the beautiful woven garden, my heart pounding with indecision, and closed my eyes to the shimmering swirl of color at my feet. Then I heard the winged flower's luminescent green anther call my name again, not in a hushed tone, but in a low mournful melody.

"How much?" I asked in something just above a whisper, silently praying his answer would be a number I could afford.

***

A mist covered the hills around the house the day my father came home to tell my mother the news. She went to the window when she heard the gate open, but only saw his outline, a form shaded grey by air heavy with moisture. Fatima, my father's favorite ewe, padded across the newly damp soil and tucked her head between the wooden slats of her pen to nuzzle his outstretched hand.

My mother said my father looked to her at the window, his eyes wide with unshed tears, and she knew without words.

The Revolution had come to our hills.

***

I went to Baku to research the story, Ali and Nino, by Kurban Said. A tale of true love with a poignant message. I stayed in Baku because a small independent news agency needed an English language editor.

The agency operated from a pre-revolutionary flat at the top of a flight of broken stairs, off a neglected courtyard in the teeming city center of Baku. Each afternoon I dodged rows of daily laundry strung between ancient windows to get to the entrance. On the other side of the front door, activity hummed a serious tune. The large room, once an aristocrat's parlour, held no separate offices, no cubes, only beat-up desks from some long-forgotten business, and computers that worked reasonably well when the power was stable. It was a space filled with vibrant, multicultural, multilanguage people like myself dedicated to reporting the news that didn't usually get reported. A place on the edge.

And, as with most things not officially sanctioned, a place that offered little money. I managed to buy the carpet from Nagorno-Karabakh, but my emergency cash had taken a hit and I would need to be more frugal in the coming months.

My desk, flush with the far wall of the main door-less room, was sandwiched between Aziz, the staff photographer/audio guy who never spoke, and Tarana, the Russian-to-Azeri translator with a fondness for Turkish sweets, who never stopped pelting me with questions, querying about my previous evening's activities. The day after I bought the carpet was no different. She didn't even wait for me to sit. In a room full of dark-eyed, dark-haired people, I was the resident anomaly with my shock of pale hair, and, as Salima so kindly put it, weird eyes. Everyone turned to hear my answer. I kept it simple and didn't mention the winged flower with the luminescent green anther.

"I went to the old town for dinner with a friend."

She nodded, and her questions went on from there—all in Russian, the language I'd studied at university. What restaurant? What did you eat? Were there any tourists? When I struggled to answer, she reminded me she was just trying to help me polish my rusty Russian vocabulary. Speaking at least one of the local languages was an advantage in our business, and I needed all the help I could get.

Inquisition and lesson over, Tarana and I settled down to our work. This was a busy time. The elections were only two months away and an opposition party was trying, once again, to gain a foothold in the government. They wanted action, not stalemate, around issues of corruption, education reform, refugee camps, and general quality of life. At three, I took a break and switched my screen to our search engine and queried carpets from Nagorno-Karabakh. The first site mentioned they were often quite large and created in sets of three or five to decorate walls as well as floors. That didn't sound like my carpet. A second site talked about the area's unique sheep, but gave no details other than the sheep had thick coats. A third site highlighted the use of bright colors and geometric flower designs. I agreed with the bright colors, but there was nothing geometric about the flowers in my carpet. Frustrated, I wanted to know more.

Of the journalists and translators at the agency, I knew Tarana best, but her language skills were limited to Russian and Azeri and I didn't think I could muster the details of Russian to ask about carpets and the history of carpet making in the early twentieth century. Parvana, a young enthusiastic Azeri journalist who lived for politics and wanted government change, spoke Azeri, Russian, and some English. I went to her for advice. She thought for a minute, then led me down the hall past the kitchen and knocked on a partially closed door. A thin, grey-haired man I had never met sat at a desk peering at a book illuminated in the faint glow of an ancient metal lamp. Parvana spoke to him in Azeri, then turned to me.

"This is Shahim. He has been a journalist in our country for many years, and now works as our historian." I understood. He made sure the facts were truth.

Shahim stood and shook my hand. "Salam," he offered softly.

"Salam," I responded. Then, in my best Russian, with a little help from Parvana, I told him who I was and what I was interested in. Shahim glanced at his chair, but did not sit. Parvana, understanding, darted back to the other room and returned with two small stools.

Shahim's two languages, like Tarana's, were Russian and Azeri. It was an odd transfer of words, but somehow amongst the three of us, we managed. What I learned was heartbreaking and wonderful at the same time. I learned the people from the mountains of Karabakh, the ones who made my carpet, had been revered as weavers. A piece from them was a gift. Sadly, in 1921, Bolshevik victory and subsequent boundary disputes forced a number of these people to start a new life in the lowlands, far from the high mountains that inspired them. Shahim believed the sheep fared no better. Without the harsh winters, their coats grew thin and the wool lost its magic luster. I asked if anyone had tried to bring the sheep and weavers back to the hills. He told me the Soviets opened carpet schools in Shusha and a few other cities in the region in the 1930s, and again in 1950s, but it was never the same. Shahim did not know what efforts had been made since the Armenians had taken control in 1994.

For a time we sat in silence, then I pulled out my phone and showed Shahim a photo of the winged flower in my carpet. Shahim studied the photo for several minutes before pulling a book from an upper shelf. He thumbed the pages to a black-and-white photograph of a mountain meadow coated in spring blossoms. In the foreground, enlarged by the angle of the lens, a lone flower with its wing-like petals turned to the sun grew from a rocky outcrop. Slowly I moved my lips to form the sounds written in Cyrillic beneath the picture—The Khari Bulbul of Karabakh.

***

The day we were to move, my mother woke with pain. She was in her seventh month and worried I might come early just to bring more trouble into our house. Later she would tell me I was a good child, a blessing, but on that day she did not think this.

My father told her to stay in bed and began to unpack our things. My mother rested, and by noon felt better, but by then it was too late. The soldiers already stood at the garden wall. They shouted at my father, and my father pleaded back. He said we could not go just yet. We had to wait for the baby. The soldiers did not like his answer and shot Fatima in the head.

We carried Fatima in the wagon down the steep mountain road until we reached the edge of our valley and were away from the soldiers. There, my father carefully sheared her coat and buried her body at the top of a hill where a vibrant patch of Khari Bulbul reveled in the warm afternoon sun. My mother said my father stood on the hill for a long time, staring out across the land to the high mountains, not moving. Then, when the sun dipped below the horizon, he knelt before the most beautiful of the Khari Bulbul and gently touched its petals. A fine, brilliant-green powder fell from the flower's center and into the palm of his hand.

When I was old enough to understand, my mother told me there was another legend our people had of the Khari Bulbul, one told in a folk song about the Khan of Karabakh and his princess daughter who married an Iranian king. In time, the princess became sad, for she missed her home in the hills outside of Shusha. The Iranian king, who loved his beautiful wife and wanted to see her smile again, built her a vast garden at his palace in Iran planted with all the flowers of her homeland. The garden turned green and flourished—all but the Khari Bulbul, which refused to grow anywhere but in the mountain meadows of Karabakh.

My mother said my father would place his hands on her rounded belly and whisper to me. She said he called me his princess, his precious daughter who was taken from her home to live in a far away land. She said he never wanted me to be sad or melancholy like the Khan's princess daughter in the legend.

My father died the week before I was born. With Fatima's

wool dyed the brilliant green of the luminous spores of the flower of Karabakh, he finished my carpet.

***

Two weeks after I talked to Shahim, the agency asked me to cover the opposition rally being held in Azadlyq Square next to the Government House. Tarana told me not to take a camera or a cellphone, to just go and listen, then later write what I saw and what I heard. She also cautioned me to stand at the back and to cover my abnormally white hair.

The morning of the rally I awoke on my living room floor. The soft threads of my carpet's warp yarn quivered in the exhale of my breath. This was not the first time I'd fallen asleep in this manner. Since I had brought the carpet home, I had not slept anywhere but inches from the delicate, bird-winged flower, the one the Azerbaijani people named the Khari Bulbul, the bee-nightingale. Even though the flower's anther called to me each night in a whispered melody, I still had not found the courage to step across the carpet's braided-rose border and surrender myself to its fluttering, expectant, garden.

I dressed in what I wore every day. A plain collared shirt over a loose-fitting pair of slacks. Comfortable shoes. To please Tarana, I draped a dark-grey scarf over and around my hair.

I took the Boulevard to get to Azadlyq Square. In the last five years, the Azeri government had spent millions—billions--of dollars to reclaim the waterfront area along the Caspian Sea to provide an attractive open park lined with fountains, restaurants, and promenades. The changes were a great improvement to a city with a history of tar-stained beaches littered with the flotsam from centuries of sea trade and oil production. Just to the west of the Boulevard, across the five-lane Neftchilar Prospekt, stood the bold, but attractive, concrete mass of Dom Soviet, the Government House, and Azadlyq Square where thousands waited behind a barricade.

Despite my instructions, I didn't want to be at the back. Instead, I stood right in front near the guy with the megaphone. I watched and listened while the engaged, young faces of the country chanted for reform. When the crowd surged right, I flowed right. When it went left, I followed. Perhaps it was the anger, the sadness I still felt when I thought about the injustices suffered by the people from Nagorno-Karabakh, the taking of freedoms, the unfair edicts assigned by governments--I didn't know. I just knew I belonged in that crowd, that swirling mass of humanity, and that was why when the police arrived, I did not leave. When the crowd surged left again, I fell, literally, into the arms of a very surprised young officer. He grabbed my shoulders, spun me around, and fastened a zip tie to bind my wrists.

***

My mother lived to see the birth of my third grandson, the sweet round-faced treasure who still dotes on me in these twilight years. She, like my father, rests in eternity under the old tree by the stream that watered our lowland village. My husband, a hard-working farmer, survived the Soviet collectives only to die from a fever in the Karabakh relocation camp in 1994. We were a nation of displaced people living in tents and makeshift shelters. I had hoped to carry his body home, but returning to our land was not to be.

Now, I am near to my time. The hills of my people are still closed and I have accepted that I, too, will be buried in strange soil for there is no way back for me. But my father's Khari Bulbul that lived at the edge of our valley, the flower that has warmed my heart for over nine decades, need not suffer my fate. My grandson agrees with me, and I know he has been thinking. He, of all my family, understands the mastery of his great-grandfather.

***

The fading sunlight warned me hours had passed since my arrest. The agency had probably tried to locate me, but I was not officially part of their staff and I doubted what they could do for me. I was just an American on a tourist visa. An arrested American tourist. The officers had been respectful, but my crime was of a political nature, and one not easily forgiven.

I heard the murmur of voices from the outside hall, but all the others in my ward, in the cells I could not see, had gone quiet. I shifted on the hard bench and leaned my head against the wall. The pieces of green fuzz I'd gathered earlier I kept cradled in my hand. This color in my carpet, this pale, soft, luminescent green wool, was used only in the anther of the one flower, but I had gathered enough for ten anthers for ten flowers. I tightened my fist and the tiny fibers warmed my fingertips against the damp cold of my cell like a mother's breath on a child's hand. I stared at the locked metal door, then let my gaze wander over the stark walls. I'd heard rumors of abuse in the prisons, but the only fear I felt was that I would never see my carpet again.

The groan of a sliding bolt broke my thoughts and I quickly tucked the anther's green puffs into my pocket. A pleasant-faced guard with silver temples opened the door to my cell and waved me out. I walked slowly down the hall to where a man in a white shirt and blue slacks stood and handed me a crumpled plastic grocery bag. Inside were my scarf, watch, and lip balm.

The guard with the silver temples then motioned me toward a door at the end of the hall where another officer, this one in a dark military uniform, waited until I was less than a meter from him before pressing the buzzer that released the lock. I hesitated, then stepped across the threshold into a room that screamed freedom. The prison door closed quietly behind me. There were no words spoken, no papers signed. I stood awkwardly erect and scanned the room for Tarana, but she was not there.

A movement to the right caught my eye. An elderly stooped woman with a bright blue patterned scarf tied over her hair struggled to her feet. She was tiny and wrinkled. The man sitting beside her rose and offered her his arm. I wondered whom they had come to see, then realized I had met him before. He was Ramil, the carpet dealer.

I froze, rigid, as my pocket suddenly burned against my skin.

"Please," Ramil said to me in his soft gentle voice, "I'd like you to meet my grandmother."

But I already knew who she was. Her eyes were a pale, luminescent green.

The next day I flew to Tbilisi, then took the overnight train to Shusha. In my bag I carried the carpet from Nagorno-Karabakh—the orange and black and pink and yellow one a loving father wove for his beautiful daughter who had to grow up in a faraway land.

The one that chose me to bring it home.

TIDINGS

JAYNE MOORE WALDROP

Jayne Moore Waldrop is a writer, recovering
attorney, and recent graduate of the Murray State
University MFA Program. She lives with her family
in Lexington, Kentucky.

When Astrid Ethridge died, only a handful of nieces and nephews survived her. They asked few questions, assuming that she died of natural causes, given her age and frail, birdlike frame. Most hadn't seen her in years. The ones who maintained contact had done their best to overlook the insults and jabs that their aunt slung unmercifully in their direction, over the phone or in person. They agreed it was a blessing she hadn't suffered or lingered.

Ruthie Owens had gotten the first call a little after 7 a.m. as she dressed for work.

"I'm trying to locate the family of Astrid Ethridge," a man's voice said.

"I'm her niece. Actually, great-niece."

"Would you consider yourself Mrs. Ethridge's next-of-kin?"

"I'm not the only one, but I guess there's no one closer. Who is this?"

"I'm Dr. Baldwin in Danville and I'm sorry to give you this news over the phone. Mrs. Ethridge died early this morning at Boyle County Hospital."

"What happened?" Ruthie said. "Was she sick?" She felt a rush of guilt for not checking on Astrid. She hadn't seen or talked to her for nearly three months.

"She died in childbirth," he said.

"Could you repeat that?" Ruthie said. "My phone must

have cut out."

The doctor cleared his throat.

"Before Mrs. Ethridge died, she gave birth to a small but otherwise healthy baby boy."

Ruthie was speechless. "Are you still there, Ms. Owens?"

"This must be some sort of joke. My great-aunt is 92 years old."

"I assure you, I'm as shocked as you are. I've practiced medicine for 20 years, and I've never seen anything like it."

Ruthie didn't know what to think.

"I'm on my way," she said. She hoped it wasn't too late to get a sub for her kindergarten class at Lone Oak Elementary.

***

Must be some mistake, she thought, as she pulled on her clothes. Yet the voice on the other end had spoken with authority, the way doctors speak. Ruthie had never heard of a Dr. Baldwin. She only knew Dr. Mullins, the elderly doctor who had cared for Aunt Astrid for the past 30 years or so. She'd met him at Astrid's annual checkups. For the last few years, Ruthie had volunteered to take her aunt to those appointments rather than let her drive the old lame Cadillac in the garage. Astrid claimed that the last mechanic who worked on the car had defrauded her by sticking a screwdriver into the tires. The tires were so old they had dry rotted and wouldn't hold air, but nobody could tell her anything. After a long teaching career at a New England boarding school, Astrid didn't appreciate challenges to her authority.

Ruthie phoned the news to her husband, Joe, already at his desk in the principal's office. During school hours, he was her boss.

"Call me if you need me," he said. "You did everything you could to help her, but that was an impossible task."

"I feel bad that I didn't know she'd gotten sick," Ruthie said.

She started to tell Joe what the doctor said about a baby, but decided not to. It sounded so foolish. Suspecting the whole thing was a prank, she would see for herself if the baby actually existed. Maybe she had imagined the entire conversation with the doctor; it seemed so unreal. Perhaps she dreamed it. Her dreams were often so vivid that she woke up mad at Joe for something he hadn't even done.

Ruthie then called both of her sisters to tell them of Astrid's death. She didn't mention the baby. She worried that if she told them now, they'd think she had lost her mind or overdosed on her old prescription of clomiphene, the fertility drug she had taken for three years while trying to get pregnant. As it boosted her chances at ovulation, its hormonal effects had caused nausea, weight gain, bloating, mood swings, and a physical and mental wobbliness that wearied her of the entire topic of conception. She adopted the motto "it is what it is" when questioned about her pregnancy status each month by friends, family, and strangers in the waiting room at the fertility clinic.

"Would you mind calling the rest of the family? I need to get to the hospital," she told her sister Virginia, who was already at her downtown law office.

"Sorry you have to do this by yourself, but I guess no good deed goes unpunished," Virginia said. "You're one of the few who could stand being around her."

For years, most of them avoided contact with their great-aunt. When Astrid's name appeared on caller ID, the call was ignored or the ringer silenced. A few had continued to visit in hopes of securing an inheritance from the childless old woman. Lately, some of the cousins, especially those with young children, suggested Astrid should no longer be invited to family events. Just too unpleasant, they said.

This must be a joke, Ruthie thought as she brushed her hair and put on lipstick. A 92-year-old woman having a baby was…well, impossible. It sounded like a parable from the Bible or some ancient mythology. The kind of story that little children believed when they heard it in Sunday school, but later doubted as they became teenagers. Ruthie shook her head. Even if it could happen, even if it could be true, why would God choose someone as hateful as Astrid for a role in an act of divine intervention?

By all accounts, Astrid was unlikeable. Ugly, not in appearance, but to her core. Even her kindest neighbors dreaded seeing her unsteady approach at their front doors. She came only when she needed something, like a ride to the bank, her gutters cleaned, or the pilot light on her stove checked. If she didn't need anything, she treated them as inferiors. The old woman had outlived five siblings and three husbands. Some people surmised that two of the three husbands died just to get out of their misery.

Ruthie collected her coat and purse, grabbed her sack lunch from the refrigerator, and headed to the nearly-new small SUV parked in the garage. They chose it because they wanted a car big enough to haul cargo and people, but they felt silly buying a mini-van. It would have made their pregnancy watch even more obvious. To everyone.

For years, Ruthie had wanted a baby more than anything. Each month she watched for signs, the ones she lived for: like her body temperature, telling her when an egg was moving, making its journey toward possible conception. On those days, she grabbed Joe as soon as he walked in the door. A few weeks later, she waited and longed for other signs—tenderness in her breasts, a sensation deep inside telling her that something had caught hold. She prayed to God, and at times she was convinced she could feel it happening. But each month, her dreams were flushed away.

Right before her last birthday, Ruthie had accepted that she probably wouldn't ever get pregnant. She told herself it was okay. She and Joe talked about adoption, but they hadn't made any decisions. They would've made good parents, she knew. She loved Joe. They had a strong marriage that could survive the disappointment. She loved her teaching job. She was close to her sisters' kids, all conceived without much fanfare. It was what it was.

***

She navigated the maze of streets and cul-de-sacs in Town Branch subdivision where they had built their new three-bedroom house a few years ago. Lexington's south end, filled with young families living in dream homes on the outskirts of town, was jammed this time of day with people heading to work and school. Long lines of cars, waiting to drop off kids, parked along the curb in front of the nearby elementary. Ruthie wondered if anyone rode school buses anymore.

After she passed the county line, her twenty-mile drive to Danville traversed a barren landscape. The old road was lined with ancient stone walls that encircled forlorn homeplaces and decrepit outbuildings, no longer producing crops or live-stock. The new four-lane on the other side of the county had fallowed this stretch of road. Fields orange with broom sedge were sprinkled with ragged-bark cedars, and patches of snow remained from last weekend's light dusting. She passed an abandoned fruit stand and a gas station with prices posted, dating its demise.

Ruthie's thoughts returned to the baby. It sounded ridiculous. Perhaps a confused teenage mother panicked and abandoned a baby near the bed where Astrid lay dying. Otherwise, this story was big. Virgin birth was one thing—at least the Virgin Mary had been of childbearing age. Aunt Astrid was ninety-two, for Pete's sake. No way her biological clock was still ticking. At 38, Ruthie herself was consumed with the quiet, steady ticking of her own body parts. In the ticking, she thought she heard a whisper: "Not this time. Not this time. Maybe next time." She had grown sick of its tease.

Her thoughts moved to Astrid. For a long time, Ruthie cared for her aunt out of some sense of moral obligation, due either to her belief in a higher power or at least her loyalty to her family. Even as unlikeable as Astrid was, Ruthie told herself, family was family. Some had to be taken care of. Ruthie felt sorry for her aunt, alone, with no one to care for her and no one to love her. Please, God, don't let me end up like Astrid.

A few months back, on a bright fall Sunday afternoon, Ruthie went to check on Astrid. It turned out to be her last visit. Since Astrid didn't drive and she wouldn't hire help, Ruthie never knew if there was food in the house. Each time she visited, she took a supply of staples: grocery bags filled with fresh fruit, skim milk and plain shredded wheat. The groceries had to be low fat, low sodium and low calorie or Astrid would throw them out. She considered herself an authority on nutrition. Weight gain was yet another sign of inferiority.

"Come in. Take a seat on the sofa," Astrid said, steering her into the living room. "Let me turn on a few lights."

Drapes and shades were closed, blocking the light of the sun. The house was silent, with no music or sound of voices, live or from a television. The furnishings hadn't changed since Ruthie used to come as a child with her parents on their obligatory visits. A gold brocade sofa, nearly as long as the old Cadillac, sat on avocado green sculpted carpet. A familiar silk floral arrangement, at least thirty years old and dusty, sat on a marble-topped table. On one wall of the adjoining dining room was a wallpaper mural, an autumnal scene of what looked like a small New England town, any inherent quaintness lost in its unnaturally bright shades of orange, red and gold.

The only change to the rooms was the amount of clutter on every available surface, including the dining room table. Astrid couldn't bear to part with anything. Treasured family pieces—a mantel clock and a gold-framed photograph of Ruthie's great-grandmother—were stacked next to plastic grocery bags filled with empty, rinsed milk cartons and years of LL Bean catalogs. At some point Astrid transformed from curator of family memorabilia to hoarder. She closed herself off in the spacious house, alone, a shuttered museum to herself.

Despite the clutter, Astrid herself looked well-groomed and stronger than when Ruthie last saw her. She wore an attractive beige sweater with a triple-row pearl necklace. Her hair color, Frivolous Fawn, hadn't changed in years. No gray roots showed. Ruthie saw a hint of how Astrid might have looked as a younger woman.

She sat down on the sofa next to Ruthie and inspected her over reading glasses. She passed her hand along Ruthie's back, a movement something like an affectionate pat, but the fingers hesitated, lingering along where Ruthie's bra strap hooked. Ruthie felt the fingers as they measured the small amount of back fat that bulged against the strap.

"Have you put on weight?" Astrid said.

"A little. It's a side effect of the fertility drugs." Ruthie knew her face looked round and puffy and her body felt thick and full while she was on the drugs. She didn't like the way she felt or looked, but she tried not to think about it. If she got pregnant, it was worth it.

"Don't let it get out of hand. No husband wants that."

Ruthie felt her cheeks get warm. The old woman had a gift for ferreting out sensitive spots.

"Joe and I want a baby. We're doing everything we can to have one. I'm not worried if I gain some weight, and Joe isn't either."

"You've just waited too long to get pregnant," Astrid said. "You're probably too old."

Ruthie's eyes filled with tears.

"We only waited until we had a nice house and Joe became principal," she said. "We didn't mean to wait too long."

Astrid's expression changed as she stared at Ruthie. Her face softened; for a moment, the scowl lines between her eyebrows disappeared.

"There's never a perfect time," Astrid said, looking around the room and focusing on an oil painting of her first husband. His face appeared young and healthy, but he had died at 34 of a massive heart attack. A congenital defect they never knew he had.

"The doctor says the odds are pretty good," Ruthie said. "It could still happen."

Astrid's voice snapped back to her usual sharpness. "It's no use. You're just like me. God didn't want us to have children."

Ruthie didn't know which part of the conversation stung more: that God was actively involved in denying her a baby or that she might actually be like Astrid. Even though they shared common genes, Ruthie never wanted to be like her. Cruel. Selfish. Alone. But she wondered if her aunt was right. Was it too late for a baby? Was she a younger version of Astrid? Both thoughts hobbled Ruthie.

When she returned home and described the conversation to Joe, he hugged her and suggested she not go back.

"She's mean. And she's wrong. Why subject yourself to it?" he said. She took his advice. She hadn't been to Astrid's house in months.

She pondered that last conversation, though, for weeks. She cried when she thought that her failure to get pregnant was an act of God's punishment, not a matter of physiology. Why would God punish her? What had she done to deserve it? If Astrid was right, God had already decided and nothing would change God's will. That was when she quit taking the hormones, telling herself it was hopeless to intervene.

She just hadn't told Joe yet.

Astrid's assessment that the two were alike was even more unsettling. Ruthie was terrified by the possibility. She asked her sisters.

"Don't be silly," Jan said. "You're nothing like her."

Ruthie wasn't so sure. She knew that her sisters were nothing like Astrid. Virginia was a lawyer and Jan was a dental hygienist. They hadn't chosen teaching as a profession. Her sisters had gotten pregnant without effort. They lived in houses teeming with children, friends and pets. In many ways, Jan and Virginia were alike, but Ruthie had always felt different from them—quieter, more private, and now, filled with more doubt than she ever suspected of her sisters.

***

As she got closer to Danville, Ruthie noticed a lighted sign warning of ice on the high bridge that crossed the Kentucky River. She slowed to avoid any slick patches. She glimpsed the gorge's limestone walls, from which hung giant icicles that grew in areas blocked from the sun's light and warmth by an adjacent hilltop. One side of the river's walls remained in perpetual shadow, allowing the ice to survive until spring; the side that received sunlight was dotted with plants and shrubs that managed to germinate and cling to the inhospitable rock ledges.

Once in town, she made her way into the parking lot of the hospital, an old-fashioned downtown hulk of red brick, with the regular placement of large windows that suggested it was a hospital or courthouse or other public building. She found a parking spot and headed to the front door. The lobby smelled like spray disinfectant. A man worked a large buffer across the terrazzo floors.

"I'm here to see Dr. Baldwin. Can you page him for me?" Ruthie said to the receptionist at the front desk. The neatly dressed woman wore a ribbon badge that read Corrine W. 20 Years of Volunteer Service.

"I'm not allowed to page doctors, but I'll call up to labor-and-delivery to see if he's still in the hospital," Corrine said.

"Labor-and-delivery?" Ruthie said.

"Yes, second floor. That's where he works," Corrine said as she picked up the phone and dialed.

Maybe it's not a prank, Ruthie thought. The receptionist hung up.

"Dr. Baldwin is waiting for you in Room 314," she said. "Take the first set of elevators."

***

On the third floor, Ruthie stopped at the nurses' station and asked for directions to Room 314. Instantly, the chatter stopped. A young nurse stood up and quietly said, "I'll take you there." She motioned for Ruthie to follow down the hall. Ruthie saw room after room filled with very sick, very old people. The doors were propped open, allowing no privacy. This was not the floor where new life came into the world. This was the floor where they ushered out the old, the sick, the dying.

The nurse stopped at 314, opened the door but stayed in the hall. A sign placed on the door read Do Not Enter. Ruthie wondered if the room was quarantined, like in the old days with tuberculosis and other contagious diseases. She walked in, and the nurse pulled the door shut.

The room was darkened. The florescent ceiling lights were off; natural light streamed through the large window. A man sat near the window, a patient file in his lap.

"Ms. Owens?" the man said as he stood to greet her. Ruthie nodded and shook his hand.

"I'm Dr. Baldwin. Have a seat," he said, motioning to one of two orange leatherette chairs. His white coat was embroidered with a dark red script—Dr. Daniel Baldwin OB/GYN. He looked tired, yet seemed anxious to talk.

Ruthie sat down, in clear view of her aunt's body, lying in a hospital bed that had been cranked to flatness. Astrid looked tiny and frail, pale and white. Shrouded in the stiff, bleached hospital linens, silenced and still, the body bore little resemblance to the living Astrid. Ruthie had never seen her look peaceful, but her body looked almost angelic, her white hair smoothed along her small head, her skin just a few shades deeper. So much had changed about her, Ruthie thought, not just the fact that she was dead. What had gone on in this room? What had gone on inside this body?

"Ms. Owens, I'm not sure where to begin. First, I'm sorry about your aunt's death but I want to assure you that I've tried to maintain privacy on what has happened here. That's why the sign's on the door."

Ruthie nodded.

"Your aunt came into the hospital because she was feeling faint. She called 911 from her home late last night."

"I had no idea," Ruthie said. "I would have been here if I'd known."

"We contacted you as soon as possible. Your name and number were the only ones we found in her purse."

Ruthie was sorry that her aunt had died alone.

"She was conscious when EMS workers arrived at her house.

She told them that she had a lot of pain in her lower abdomen, and that she was short of breath. She also seemed somewhat delusional."

"Really? She's always had a sharp mind."

"She told them that a woman had been at her house caring for her for the past few weeks. Apparently the woman's a nurse, but she told your aunt to call 911 because there was nothing more she could do," Dr. Baldwin said.

"A woman helping her? I have no idea who that could be," Ruthie said. The family had tried for years to convince Astrid to get help or move out of that big house. She wouldn't hear of it.

"She described the woman as having dark skin. Not in those exact words," the doctor said. He hesitated for a moment, as though he didn't want to tell the rest. "All night she called out racial epithets, telling me to get the dark-skinned woman out of the room."

Ruthie frowned. She knew the word Dr. Baldwin was avoiding. The n-word. Her aunt had started using it again. Astrid hadn't always used it. She was an educated woman, a teacher at one of the most prestigious boarding schools in the country, back in the day when some of the Kennedy and Rockefeller boys went there. During her years in New England, Astrid had erased her Kentucky drawl and any vestige of open racial prejudice. After she retired, she moved to Danville, where she was respected for a career spent educating America's brightest young minds. She had a fine reputation. But recently, she had moments when she seemed to transport back to when she was a young woman, living in the small town where she grew up near the Tennessee border, where generations of her family had relied on the word to maintain order.

Ruthie and her cousins had a hint that something might be wrong with Astrid when she cussed them at last year's Fourth of July picnic, even her favorite nephew, the Methodist preacher. She called them all whores and bastards. Astrid had never kept her opinions to herself, but the change was in her choice of words. She'd never tolerated profanity or vulgarity in her classroom or home, but lately, she had taunted them at family gatherings by cursing and even using the n-word. In front of the youngest children, too. Protests seemed to egg her on, so she said them more frequently and threw in additional slurs about Catholics and Jews. Ruthie wondered if a form of dementia could make her elderly aunt revert to bigotry, expressed with a lilting southern accent. For the past few years, the family had witnessed the unfiltered, private ugliness of Astrid, after a lifetime of seeing the polished public version.

Without realizing it, Ruthie swiped her tongue across her front teeth and remembered a taste from childhood. She— and her sisters—learned that speaking the n-word and other bad words was not tolerated by their parents. Some of the kids at school said it on the playground, but Ruthie learned that such talk was cause for a mouth-washing with a bitter, highly perfumed soap that their mother kept for such occasions. A small motel soap bar fit directly into their child mouths, scraped across their baby teeth and left a waxy residue to remind them of their ugly talk for the rest of the day. Ruthie never forgot that taste. And she never said the word.

"I'm sorry that she spoke like that to one of your nurses," Ruthie said.

"You need to know that none of us saw the dark-skinned woman she spoke of. Plus, your aunt was talking directly to this woman when she came into the emergency room. She called her Gabriella."

"I've never heard of her."

Ruthie wondered if Aunt Astrid had been delirious. Maybe it was a dream that seemed real, Ruthie thought. Like her own.

The doctor said that he'd delivered a baby earlier in the evening and was preparing to leave the hospital when he noticed how crowded the emergency room entrance was. Multiple ambulances. A wreck out on the main road. Lots of injuries. The staff was overwhelmed. The head of the emergency room, a friend since med school, asked him if he could stick around and help.

"Your aunt arrived in yet another ambulance, writhing in pain and holding her swollen lower abdomen. A nurse—a redhead I'd never seen before—met the paramedics as they rolled her in. The EMS suspected a large pelvic tumor. Her vitals were strong, though. The nurse said there were no more beds in the emergency room but that she'd find another room for her."

He had followed the nurse down the hall, then up the elevator to this room.

"Your aunt was quiet as we passed through the hallways and when I started to examine her, but her pain returned in a few minutes. It was rhythmic, like labor, but at her age, I never gave it a second thought. Her abdomen had the tautness of full-term pregnancy, but I kept thinking tumor. The nurse was adjusting the stirrups for a pelvic exam and when I rested my hand on her belly, I felt movement. Unquestionably, a baby." Dr. Baldwin looked like a first-year med student as he told the story.

Ruthie remained silent. How could this be? This tiny, flattened body had just been through labor? Astrid hadn't looked strong enough to endure childbirth any time in Ruthie's memory. What had happened to the firm roundness the doctor had described? She remembered her sisters' pregnancies, when their bellies moved to reveal each jab by their impatient babies, ready to be born. She also knew it took days, weeks, even months for those bellies to flatten and constrict, but Astrid's body had already returned to fragility, its thin skin stretched across weakening bone, with no sign of lush, recent fertility.

"I didn't know what I was dealing with," he said. "I was working with only the one nurse. The redhead, the one with the blue eyes. She was very good, maybe a midwife. There were times when she seemed more in control of the situation than me."

Ruthie listened as he described the birth. And the death.

"I wanted to get your aunt something for the pain but the baby was coming too quickly. I had assumed that her extreme muscle atrophy—entirely consistent with her age—would keep her from having the strength to be able to push. I was wrong. She pushed hard and almost silently, except for talking to the woman she called Gabriella until the baby was delivered."

The baby was born at 3 a.m. Astrid died within minutes.

"She continued to talk to Gabriella, more calmly than before. She had no sign of hemorrhaging but her blood pressure and pulse slowed and weakened. She died quietly, very much like any 92-year-old who dies of natural causes."

He looked at Ruthie and shook his head. "If I hadn't been there, delivering this baby, I would never believe this story."

"Where's the baby? Is it alive?"

"He's fine. A little small, but he's healthy. He cried at first, like he should, then he calmed down. He looked at me like even he understands it's a miracle."

He paused and ran his hands through his hair. "I'm required by law to order an autopsy when there's a death of unknown circumstances, but I'm not sure anyone could keep this quiet if the pathologist learns that this woman died in childbirth."

There was silence. Ruthie didn't know what to say.

"Ms. Owens, I've been sitting here since the delivery, trying to decide what to do," he said. "If news of this birth leaks out, he won't have a chance at a normal life."

At this point Ruthie was only thinking about the baby.

"Do what you have to do, I guess," Ruthie said. "Can I see him? Does he look…normal?"

"Perfectly normal. Apgar scores at 9. Come on, I'll take you to the nursery on the second floor."

They walked down a flight of stairs and through buffed tile halls. At an intersection where the halls crossed, there were nursery windows and lots of activity. Nurses in scrubs were rushing around. Plastic, rolling bassinets were being shuttled to mothers' rooms for feedings and visits. Some were rolled back to the nursery to allow moms to sleep. Grandparents escorted young children arriving to see newborn siblings for the first time. Ruthie caught glimpses inside rooms, where new parents held tiny babies, faces aglow in the wonder of the moment.

"He's right here," Dr. Baldwin said, pointing to a solitary bassinet behind the glass. The baby inside wore a tiny blue sock cap and was swaddled in a light blue blanket. The sign near his feet said "Baby Boy Roe" and nothing else. No mother, no father, no details.

"I decided not to put any information on the card. For privacy reasons," he said.

"Why, he's beautiful," Ruthie said. There was a tightness in her throat that wouldn't go away with swallowing. Months ago she had dreamed of a tow-headed toddler, shrieking and laughing as he ran. Could this be him?

"He is, indeed," Dr. Baldwin said. "Would you like to hold him?"

She nodded, unable to speak.

"You're welcome to use the private room over here, next to

the nursery. I'll ask the nurses to bring you some scrubs to wear," he said. "We need to watch him for the next few hours to make sure he's okay."

He led her through a door marked Family Room, a small cubicle attached to the nursery.

"This is for families with a preemie or a sick baby. It gives them a chance to be together without going too far from newborn intensive care," Dr. Baldwin said. "Don't worry. He shows no sign of complications. I'm just being cautious."

He hesitated.

"One more detail. Have you decided on a funeral home? We need to know where the body should be sent," he said.

"Morefield's, here in Danville," she said. For years, Astrid had made it clear that she despised that tacky new funeral home built on the edge of town, wedged between the gigantic Southwest Bible Church and Wal*Mart. Astrid preferred the staid traditions and downtown location of Morefield's.

"We'll let them know. I'll check back with you after you've seen the baby," he said and left the room.

A suit of hospital scrubs sat on the small glass-top table. Ruthie put them on over her work clothes and tapped the hand sanitizer dispenser on the wall. She sat in the painted rocking chair and waited. The clock on the wall, with a face that advertised infant formula, ticked softly. It was 10 a.m.

Ruthie panicked. She had forgotten to remind Joe that her substitute teacher had to wait with Maggie Sparks at dismissal. Maggie's dad was often late to pick her up. She called Joe but got his voice mail.

"Joe, I'm still in Danville. It's been a crazy morning. There are some details I need to sort out before I can leave," she paused, considering whether to mention the baby. She decided to wait until after she held him. Then she'd know what to do.

"Please make sure the sub knows to wait with Maggie Sparks. She gets very upset if she has to wait by herself. I'll call you when I'm on my way home."

As she put the phone back into her purse, a nurse opened the inner door that led directly from the nursery. She rolled in the bassinet with the baby sleeping inside. The nurse picked him up, cradled him to her chest for a moment, and looked at Ruthie as she passed the baby.

"Here's your sweet boy," she said. Ruthie was surprised that the nurse thought he belonged to her.

Being careful to support the baby's head, Ruthie took him into her arms. She wanted to see him, to make sure he wasn't freakish, like his birth. She counted his toes and fingers, felt the curvature of his head, and listened for his breaths. How could something so beautiful come from someone like Astrid? She smelled his newness, unlike anything she had smelled before. She had never before held a baby so new. She didn't know how he had come to be in her arms, but it felt so natural.

The clock on the wall ticked as Ruthie rocked the boy. There was a light tap on the door and Dr. Baldwin walked in.

"How's he doing?"

"He's perfect," Ruthie said. The doctor smiled and nodded.

"Ms. Owens, I hope you understand that, if this story gets out, he's going to be hounded for life."

"Won't the privacy rules protect him?"

"Normally, yes, but this isn't a normal event. I can't guarantee that the news won't get out. There won't be an autopsy, unless you insist." Ruthie shook her head.

"I appreciate you trying to keep it quiet. It is what it is, I suppose."

"I want to protect him. I believe that's what I'm supposed to do. I'm sure you do, too."

Dr. Baldwin paced in the little room, so small that he crossed it in two or three strides.

"And, we've got an immediate problem. Who's going to take this baby home? I'd hate to see him go into foster care, if he has a family," he said.

The question surprised Ruthie. Until that moment, she had been immersed in the baby. She hadn't considered anything beyond the walls of the tiny room. Not even Joe.

"He's one of us. We're Astrid's family. We'll do what's right," she said. She saw Dr. Baldwin's eyes studying the rings on her left hand.

"Do you have children, Mrs. Owens?"

"Not yet. We're still trying."

He nodded, and paused before he spoke again.

"I don't understand how this baby came into the world. Usually that's the easiest question I get to explain to my patients," he said. "And I don't know why he came into the world. The only thing I know for certain is that he's here and he deserves to be loved, just like any other new baby. No more and no less than the others."

He opened the door, and turned back toward Ruthie. "Just think about it."

She nodded and kept rocking. She didn't want to think of the world outside. There would be so many questions.

Holding him close, she fed him from a small glass bottle of formula that had been left in the corner of the bassinet. Her mind went back to Astrid. She wondered about what had happened in her great-aunt's life in the past few months. She thought about what had gone on in Astrid's life for as long as she'd known her. Ruthie grappled with the mystery of how the old woman became the link between hope and fulfillment, the bridge between heaven and earth.

The clock ticked as they rocked; she ran her hand lightly over his small peach-fuzzed head. Another hour passed. A different nurse came in to check on them, but Ruthie hardly noticed. He was sleeping and she didn't want to wake him. She was mesmerized with the baby, his breathing, the rocking, the ticking.

"Would you like for me to take him back?" the nurse whispered. Ruthie looked up, into eyes that were a color she'd not seen before, a glittering swirl of aquamarine, azure, and turquoise. The nurse's red hair was pulled back into a ponytail, her freckled face attentive and eager, yet comforting.

"Please, let me keep him."

"Is that what you want?"

"Yes. Just a bit longer," Ruthie said. Her gaze returned to the baby. After a few more rocking movements, she asked, "How long can I stay here?"

There was no response. Ruthie looked around and found that the nurse was gone. She and the baby were alone again. Perhaps another shift change, she thought. She must have lost track of time. She remembered she hadn't eaten since breakfast, the forgotten sack lunch still in her bag. How would she explain the baby to Joe? He might think she had done something drastic, like kidnap a stranger's baby.

Another nurse came in, announcing that she had just come on duty.

"Your baby's beautiful," she said. "I see you've decided on a name."

Ruthie started to correct her, but decided against it.

"Thank you. Well, I'm not really sure of his name yet, though."

"I was told to go through dismissal procedures with you as soon as there's a name on the birth certificate," the nurse said.

"Who said it was time for us to be dismissed?" Ruthie asked.

"Well, the birth certificate application has been signed by Dr. Baldwin. I guess one of the nurses from the last shift left a note, saying everything was in order. I need to go over the self-care instructions with you and show you how to take care of his cord and schedule his PKU test. Are you going to nurse?"

The question startled Ruthie.

"Can I see the birth certificate, please?"

"Certainly," the nurse said as she rifled through the paper-work. She pulled out a sheet and handed it to Ruthie. "Do you need a car seat? We'll give you one, no charge, if you need it."

Ruthie scanned the birth certificate application, signed by Dr. Dan Baldwin with the time of birth, weight and length filled in. So were all the other spaces.

Name of Infant: Ethridge Owens
Name of Mother: Ruthie Owens

She was startled to see her own name, in print, listed as his mother. This wasn't how she had expected to become a parent. But, she thought, nothing about having a baby had gone according to plan.

She saw, stapled to the birth certificate, an envelope with her name handwritten on it.

"Would you hold him for me?" she said to the nurse, who took the baby and stood nearby.

Ruthie opened the envelope. Inside was a copy of Astrid's death certificate, also signed by Dr. Baldwin. Under cause of death, "unspecified natural causes." She slipped it back into the envelope and tucked it in her bag.

The nurse handed the baby back to her, then gave her paper after paper, in preparation of discharging the baby from the hospital. She was nervous. It was happening so fast, but she wasn't stopping.

"Excuse me, but I noticed a small oversight on the application for his birth certificate. Would it be a big deal to fill in one blank?" she asked the nurse. She wouldn't push if doing so alerted the nurse of an irregularity. She watched the young woman's face.

"Not a problem. The doctor signed electronically. We fill in spaces all the time, like adding the baby's name."

"Perfect. I noticed my husband's name was left off. Can you add it in, where it says 'Name of Father'"?

"Oh, sure. I'm so sorry. I didn't realize we'd left it off."

"Joseph Owens is his name. I'll wait here while you fix it."

"It won't take a minute," the nurse said, heading out the door to the nurses' station.

Ruthie held the baby and rocked. She dreaded the questions that were sure to come from Joe, her sisters, everyone. As she bent down to kiss his head, he opened his puffy, blue-gray eyes and seemed to focus on her. They looked at each other for a long while. His hand, tightly clinched as if ready to fight, unfolded slightly as her forefinger touched his palm. He grasped it and didn't let go. Ruthie had her answer.

PLANET, PAPER, SPACE
MELISSA EMBRY

Melissa Embry is a former journalist living in Dallas, Texas. Her short fiction has appeared most recently in *The Lorelei Signal* and *Eternal Haunted Summer*.

The shuttle's airlock frames the orbiting station Gaia, bright against blackness, the cable between it and the shuttle stretching like a tightrope, maybe fifty meters. It looks long as eternity.

I open my palm to release my signature artwork, an origami dove, one of those that always open my installations. I turn both viewports of my helmet toward the dove, hovering in silhouette against the airless void. Got to be sure both the forward and dorsal cameras pick it up. Then I clutch the cable in both hands. Thank god the camera's electrodes are synaptically controlled. I think about taking my hands off the cable's synthetic umbilical cord even for an instant. A sudden burst of sweat drenches me under my spacesuit. With a low hum of vibration, the humidity controls whisk me dry.

"Is it still falling when it's this far up?"

"Don't worry, sir." The shuttle crew member waiting beside me clips a link from my suit to the cable. How many space tourists has she conducted along this same adventure? "You can't fall. Your auto safe will bring you in."

Reel me in like a fish? I step off the shuttle's bay, into the void.

"Captain Nguyen of Gaia here, Mr. Villafranca." A Texas drawl crackles in my headset. "You're doing fine, sir. Just don't look down."

"Thanks, captain." I open my eyes. When had I closed them?

Had the captain been able to see that through my faceplate? "I can't even tell which way down is."

"An astute observation. At this altitude, planetary gravity is too slight to register on our proprioceptors. But do me the favor of taking a deep breath. Your blood O2 level's kind of low."

"Nothing like a good whiff of canned air to put things in perspective." I look back toward the shuttle. Already I'm several meters away. Another surge of panic. But the origami dove I set free floats beside me. How can that happen when we're traveling god knows how fast? There. It's caught in the shoulder joint of my suit. I take one hand off the cable, flick the dove loose. It vanishes from sight.

"Four hundred kilometers," I whisper.

"Sir?" Nguyen again.

"Trying to remembering how far I am from Earth, captain."

"Actually, Mr. Villafranca, you're just over four hundred and seventeen klicks out. Gaia's slightly below you."

"So I'm up? And you're down?" I stare along the cable toward Gaia. Then, beyond her eclipse, I see my home planet in its blue veil of sky.

"Breathe, Mr. Villafranca, breathe."

I wave to Gaia, to Nguyen, invisibly watching me.

I take my other hand off the cable. I knew I wouldn't fall, but knowing is one thing, reality is another. There's no rush of wind to give me the feel of motion. My pressurized suit keeps the emptiness of space at bay. I'm free, free as a bird. I laugh.

"Mr. Villafranca, you all right?" the voice in my headset asks.

I take hold of the anchoring cable again and swung back and forth to give the camera implanted in the back of my head a three-sixty view through the helmet's dorsal viewport. I'd rehearsed a shooting schedule before leaving the shuttle. Now, on the inspiration of the moment, I twirl, my movements at once constrained by the bulky spacesuit and wonderfully freed from the limitation of gravity.

I kick. Against what? I spin hand over hand, the cable a pole I can vault over.

Now I'm dizzy, a purely emotional reaction. My orientation shouldn't matter to the flow of blood within my body, should it? I'm cradled by my suit like a child in the womb.

"Mr. Villafranca, you must come aboard." The voice in the headset. Then softer, like the captain damped the volume without realizing it's still on, "Jesus, we've got ourselves a head case out there."

"Sorry, captain. It's just so wonderful. I couldn't imagine."

The headset cuts out completely, probably letting Gaia's captain express himself in ways he doesn't want transmitted to mission control.

"Yes, Mr. Villafranca, it's wonderful." Nguyen's lost his drawl completely. "But we've got two vehicles trying to stay synched at twenty-seven hundred kph, and we don't want to leave anybody behind. So we'd all appreciate you coming aboard. Pronto."

***

"Captain Nguyen, I presume?"

I'm bobbing gently in the microgravity of the Gaia's closed airlock, helmet unclipped. I reach for the captain's hand, miss, start to upend. "Sorry. Haven't got my space legs yet."

The captain steadies me. "Welcome aboard, Mr. Villafranca."

"Call me Max. Hope I'm not the worst passenger you've had."

"No, sir, not at all. At least you got your own ass–excuse the language, purely a technical phrase—got across the cable on your own power. There's been some we had to sedate and haul in."

"It probably is a nuisance, me dropping in like a tourist."

"Not a tourist, Mr. Villafranca, that is, Max. A partner. Although you're the first artist we've had on board Gaia. And I've got to say, that's quite a tattoo you've got there."

"Want a closer look? Designed it myself. They had to shave my head for the camera implant so I thought, hey, why not tattoo another face around the camera port?"

I turn. "Smile, captain." I imagine a click of the tiny shutter, the look on Nguyen's face as the camera lens nestled within the Cyclops design on the back of my skull winks a picture.

***

An hour after the 2330 start of the scheduled sleep period, I'm still awake in my sleeping booth. Between my body's reluctance to adjust to the Coordinated Universal Time of the station and the thrill of being in space, I can't close my eyes.

The private booths where crew members tether their sleeping bags have viewport coverings to simulate darkness for the sleep cycle's duration. Nguyen and I had another clash over my window covering, but I'm determined not to black out my view of the planet, the almost hourly sunrise and sunsets. After all, I paid for this view. Now I lay here watching the changing sunlight from the planet's surface reflect off the sheet of paper I'm folding.

"Head case still awake?" Nguyen's voice outside my booth, pitched too low for the sleeping crew to hear but loud enough, I suspect deliberately, to carry to my ears.

"Not sure, sir." The duty's officer's voice.

"If he stays awake for the duration he really will go crazy."

I concentrate on the tiny paper sculpture forming under my fingers. After so many years, the sight of the first downward fold, the resulting triangle, is enough to induce a meditative state. Six more folds, two repeated. I open my fingers, set the bird free. It hovers in the viewport's frame.

Outside my booth, I hear fragments of the conversation.

"Sir, he's an artist," the duty officer says, answering some question of the captain's that I missed.

"Artist? Have you seen the holos of his so-called art? Dropping whatever those little paper things are—"

"Origami, sir."

"You call it origami, I call it salami."

"Dropping them into what? Volcanoes? Tsunamis? That one with the tornado gave me the creeps. If I was one of those little birds, I wouldn't like it one bit."

"It helps pay the bills, sir."

"I tell you what, one of these days there'll be an incident with these tourists we take on board to pay the bills." Nguyen emphasizes the last words. "And then there'll be hell to pay."

Silence. I imagine Nguyen crawling into his own sleeping booth. Well, he only has to put up with me for two weeks. And my next installation will be incredible. Ideas flood my brain like the changing light from my planet-side viewport. I do need to rest, though. I fold another sheet of paper, loose a second dove. It sways in the air current from the HVAC system, hovering beside the first dove, their beaks touching as if they kiss.

In the stillness of the sleeping Gaia, I feel the minute vibrations of my dorsal camera clicking automatically, one a second, every second of the day and night, or what passes for day and night on a space station.

My eyelids are heavy now. "Goodnight, my darlings," I whisper to the birds.

The next morning, rather the beginning of the next wake cycle, the floating doves greet me. Their paper wings shine in the light of sunrise, or is it sunset? A half dozen of them. Or seven or eight. I count them, then shake my head. Yesterday's spacewalk must have taken more out of me than I'd realized. I don't remember making so many.

"Probably folded you in my sleep," I say to the doves. Why couldn't I, after so many years of practice?

The puff of air from my breath sets the birds nodding in agreement.

I dress and slip out of the booth. The mild turbulence of my movement sends one of the doves fluttering out into Gaia's common area.

"Is this yours, Mr. Villafranca?" Nguyen hovers in front of me, holding a paper bird pinched between thumb and forefinger.

He's determined not to be on a first name basis with me.

I take the bird from the captain's hand, toss it into my sleeping booth, and shut the door. "Thanks. It must have gotten loose when I opened the door just now."

"It?"

I turn back to face Nguyen. A swarm of origami doves surrounds him. He swats them like flies.

"So your crew does origami, too?" I pluck a dove from the captain's shoulder. "If I didn't know better, I'd swear this was one I folded. The exact paper I use."

"Is this a joke?" Nguyen asks. "These things are all over the Gaia. Herrera found one in his toothpaste container. They're so thick we can hardly get any work done."

"Sir, captain, these aren't mine. I admit, I folded a couple, well, maybe half a dozen or so, last night. That's all."

"Mr. Villafranca, you will clean these things out immediately. You are here as a guest, not a prankster. The Gaia has serious work to do."

I pick another bird out of the air. "Captain, I did not turn all these birds loose. Obviously, someone from your crew got into my private quarters last night, took out a pack of my paper—"

Nguyen's cold as space glare stops me.

I gather a dozen tiny paper birds in my arms and turn back to my booth to shove them inside.

"They're garbage, Mr. Villafranca. Get a bag from the locker, gather all of these things, and put them in the airlock for disposal. That's an order."

The whole crew had to be in on the joke, I realize. They have to be, to have folded so many birds overnight. All except Nguyen, unless the captain is a better actor than he appears to be.

I spend most of the wake cycle capturing and bundling every bird, hundreds of them, into the Gaia's closed airlock. But except for the loss of my stock of origami paper, I can almost forgive the crew for their prank. The pictures will be terrific. Especially those of Nguyen covered in fluttering paper birds. In fact, the captain's annoyance is probably a good thing. It seems to make him forget about the camera implanted in the back of my skull. He's acting a lot less restrained than when I first arrived.

It isn't until the next sleep cycle that I have time to check my pack of origami paper. It's full except for the two sheets I remember using last night. Did the crew bring their own paper? But the birds I bagged were made out of the same brand of paper I use, the handmade paper specially stocked by my supplier. I'll have to save those garbage bags of birds from being jettisoned, get them back planetside and check every one to figure out how they managed it.

I barricade the door of my sleeping booth. That should stop any more pranks. I pull a single sheet of paper from my stock and fold. Just one folded bird, to help me sleep.

***

I wake from a nightmare of being suffocated. Only it's not a dream. I'm enveloped in a dense, crackling cloud. I spit out a wad of paper; brush more from my face, my eyes. I open my mouth to scream, to gasp for breath. A flood of wadded paper pours in. Not just wadded paper. My god, it's paper birds, origami birds just like mine. They press against me, jabbing me with the sharp points of their beaks, their wings. They're killing me. Why, why, what have I done?

I cup my hands over my face to keep them out of my nose and mouth. The mass of paper covering me fills every crevice in the sleeping booth. I kick. My feet strike the closed door. There's an answering thud from outside.

"Villafranca, open up!"

The door bursts open.

***

They've drugged me. That's the only explanation. They coaxed me on board to take my money. Now they're tired of me, they want to get rid of me. How many other passengers have they done this to?

"Psychotic break, you think? Guy should never have been taken on board." It's Nguyen and the Gaia's medic, talking softly, like they think I can't hear them, can't understand what they're doing.

I try to move. Nothing.

"How long would you say it's been since he slept?"

"Days, from the looks of him. Maybe even from before he got on the shuttle."

But I did sleep. They can't possibly think I sat up night after night folding birds. That's crazy. I lie still. As long as I keep my eyes closed, they'll think I'm unconscious. Let them.

There's nothing wrong with me. They can't make me think I'm crazy. While they had me drugged, the birds told me what's going on, what needs to be done. All I need to do now is find the proof and photograph it. The camera hidden inside my head will tell the story.

"Think we can keep him calm until the next shuttle rendezvous?" Nguyen asks. "How he managed to bring so much paper on board beats me. We don't want to take a chance of him getting hold of it again. Might have killed himself."

"By choking himself on paper? Seems a weird way to off yourself, if you ask me. Hold on, I think he's coming to."

I open my eyes, try to sit up. I scream, but only a whisper comes from between my lips. "I can't move. Why can't I move? Why can't I move?"

"It's okay, Mr. Villafranca." The medic smiles his professional smile. "You had a shock. Takes a while for all systems to come back online."

"I don't have systems. I'm a person, a human being. You think because I've got a camera imbedded in my brain—"

"Feel that?"

I curl my fingers, uncurl them. "Yeah. That's good. What did you do?"

"Nothing. You did it. Like I said, it just took some time."

"So, I'm all right?"

"Try sitting up. Feel dizzy?"

"A little."

"Micrograv does that sometimes. Take it easy for the rest of the day." Medic and captain exchange glances.

"When's the return shuttle due?" I ask. Clearly, I'm not safe around Nguyen. He's had it in for me from the first.

"Tomorrow."

"It's Tuesday already?"

"Tomorrow's Sunday, sir."

"Sunday? Is that the regular shuttle? It can't be. My god, how did that happen? You've had me unconscious for days?"

"You just lost track of time, sir. It's easy to do up here."

I close my eyes. So, I only have tonight to accomplish my task. The one the birds have set for me.

"Thanks, doc," I say. "That's reassuring. Real reassuring."

What are they trying to hide? I have the proof of what they've done, have it in my camera's memory. They've forgotten that. Or have they? Maybe they removed the memory chip while they had me sedated. It takes every bit of will power I have not to scream at the thought.

I have to examine those garbage bags in the airlock, the ones holding the origami; examine them before the Gaia jettisons the evidence. I'll need to bring back samples to prove my claims.

When Gaia's lights dim at last for the sleep cycle, I peek from my booth, its door now removed. The duty officer's back is turned. I slip into the airlock. There are so many bags of garbage. There, there were the ones I want. I rip the bags open.

The birds burst free. I try to contain them, but they elude me. They fill the airlock, pressing against every surface. They must have been multiplying while they were in the bags, even while they seemed to wait patiently within the garbage hold. They want more room. That's it. They were angry at me for confining them. They want to be free. I have to help them fly free.

I struggle against the relentless pressure of the birds, feel for the airlock's controls, find them. The outer hatch of the airlock opens. The birds burst out, exploding into the vacuum.

Poised on the outer threshold of the airlock, I watch them

leave the Gaia behind. They're a glittering cloud hovering above the rotating planet. I turn, backward, forward, feel the camera's vibration. Surely it's working. I hope the memory chip will survive to witness this last flight of my little birds. They're so beautiful. So very–

EMPIRE OF DIRT

K.B. SLUSS

KB lives in North Carolina with her kid, her husband, the occasional in-law, and a very hairy husky. She loves to read and has a sweet tooth for speculative fiction. She is a first reader for *Daily Science Fiction* and she has published short stories at *Daily Science Fiction*, *Everyday Fiction*, and *Stupefying Stories*.

Seiko waited for me at the exit of my tunnel. My other Pilot, Ahna, had already switched off her mental links and raced back to her quarters, eager for distraction after hours of mind numbing work. Keeping me under control required most of their focus. Without their constant push, I had a tendency to mutiny.

"Long day," said Seiko, who occasionally escorted me to the breedling quad. Dark circles ringed her eyes and her shoulders sagged.

I loped beside her, struggling to keep up with her long strides. *Was it?*

"You can stop thinking at me, Nanus. I'm right here."

"Habits," I said, switching the link in our connection to verbal mode. "Sorry."

"Long day when you have little to show for it."

"You got your quota."

"But all in the last half hour. This shortage is wearing on me."

"I can tell."

Seiko stopped and canted her head. "You can?"

"I don't have to see it with my eyes, you know." I tapped my temple. "It's there, like a hum in the background."

Seiko grunted.

"It's Ahna, too, isn't it?" I said.

The tips of Seiko's ears turned pink, confirming I had guessed right. "Don't say anything to her," said Seiko.

"What are you going to do?"

"You wouldn't understand, even if I could explain it."

"You might keep yourself behind a wall," I said, "but Ahna is less defensive. I know more than you think."

Seiko's face crumpled into an ugly sneer. "Second hand, Nanus. The things you glean from us are meaningless without context."

We walked in silence until we crossed the field, a barren expanse of orange silicoat dust, and entered the garage. Seiko had told me that when the first speculators arrived, the planet was so ore rich that spikes of bault literally burst from the ground. That was long before my time.

Once we reached the breedling compound, Seiko slid a stepstool to me and opened the door of my crate. "Up you go," she said.

I hesitated.

"Nanus," she said. "You still do this? To me? I won't come with you anymore. I'll just shove your mind from somewhere far away like everyone else."

I shimmied up the step ladder and crawled into the dark interior of my crate.

"Good night, Nanus," said Seiko and she locked the door behind me.

"I could think to Ahna about you. I could *insinuate* certain things, make her think they were her own thoughts."

Seiko hissed, forcing breath between clenched teeth. "I'd kill you," she said and shut down the supply to the lights. The garage went dark. When Seiko said she would kill me, her intent was genuine, but we both knew the threat was baseless. I was an exception to the breedling rule, a fortuitous twist of genetic fate, an everlasting child who never aged, never outgrew her tunnel diameters. The geneticists would keep me alive as long as it took for them to figure out how to make more just like me.

***

That night I sprawled on my sleeping mat among my small collection of possessions—a battery powered hand-lamp and a few tattered novels and books of poetry, carefully selected to encourage my complacency and cooperation. Brain anesthesia. I suspected Seiko authored a few of the poems; out of pity she had taught me to read, using these same, confining narratives.

I felt Seiko in the stories, and although she denied writing them, I once or twice caught the stains of the words in her memory. She often alluded to shadowed passageways and infinite closed doors. Eternal darkness. No escape. It was meant as a reminder for me, to keep me in my place. I didn't need the books. Without Seiko, there was nowhere I wanted to go.

I sometimes dreamed that Seiko was the one roaming those dark corridors, knocking, searching for Ahna, but she wouldn't be there. In my dreams Seiko never found her.

I put aside the books and picked up a gem of compressed silicoat the color of deep rust and completely worthless. Sometimes I found them in my tunnels and slipped them into my pocket. I slid the gem's sharp edge across the fat pad of flesh at the base of my thumb, pressing until the skin broke open around it, weeping a thick, red tear. I sometimes hurt myself like this to see if I still felt anything of my own; not something put there by my Pilots' mental suggestions.

The stones were so prolific they held no value as a jewel and couldn't be converted to fuel like bault ore. Too bad, because mining them would have kept me in work for three lifetimes. For the many years since my birth, I had resisted my purpose, but without the mines, my reason for existence ceased. And then what? Incineration if I was lucky. Salvaged and put to work in the flesh parlors if I was not.

***

The next morning I came awake on my own, not as a result of the mental alarm clock my Pilots sent me as turned on our mental connections. I was disoriented and my heart beat like an angry bee trapped behind a window. I scuttled to the end of my crate and peered out. No lights—no movement. No sound except for the snuffles of the sleeping breedlings around me.

It was a workday, but the crews were off-line. I reached out in my mind for Seiko, searching for an explanation. Without the work to prompt them, the Pilots never elected to establish connections with their breedlings, but I found her there anyway, waiting for me.

"Nanus."

At first I didn't answer her. I probed and Seiko allowed it, but only so far, letting me find the answers she didn't want to verbalize. "We're pulling out," she said.

When?

"Couple of days."

Where will you go?

Seiko sent me a likeness of an ocean—whitecaps and foam assaulting white sand beaches. She conveyed another picture: a mechanical contraption shaped like a silver tear. It sank beneath the water and settled on a sandy bottom ribbed by the flow of currents.

A robotic arm stabbed out from the teardrop, tearing a hole in the sand before a flexible pipe took its place to suck up something beneath the surface. The lifeblood of yet another planet. Behind the controls of the submersible sat a breedling, and linked to the breedling, a Pilot.

Good for you, I said, bereft of sincerity. *I feared for your unemployment.*

"Come with me," said Seiko.

I don't know anything about underwater operations. I was specifically made to withstand the rigors of tunneling and long-term exposure to bault gas.

"Nothing about you came out to spec, Nanus. I'm not asking your permission."

Doesn't matter.

"Ahna is coming, too."

She doesn't give a damn for me.

Seiko huffed her frustration. I marveled that even those little bursts of emotions managed to transmit. "It's not always about you," she said.

Doubtful of her intentions for me, I pushed into Seiko, searching for truth. She threw up a mental wall, but I rammed against it until it crumbled. Seiko shrieked, and while she struggled to recover, I ravaged her thoughts. My attack was merciless, but she knew it was a possibility when she reached out to me, alone, without Ahna to help keep me subdued.

"Nanus, stop it," she pleaded.

I ignored her, plunging further into her mental morass—there was so *much* of it. Then I found it, the soft glowing thing. The place she protected from me. The internal dwelling I never pressed to find out of my respect for her. But it was worth throwing all that away to know if she was telling the truth about taking me with her or not.

I discovered it was true, after all, that women were rare in her profession. But Seiko kept herself apart from the other

Pilots not because of her gender, but because she desired only Ahna's companionship and affections. A hundred times Seiko tried to tell her, but the words would not come. The fear that Ahna did not return the sentiment was too great. It crippled Seiko.

It made her a lot like me.

I pushed deeper and, in that place where Seiko secreted her adoration for Ahna, I found another figure, a small, familiar shape, stained orange with silicoat dust. A breedling. But it wasn't me. It was another girl, young and broken. She sat cross legged, tethered to a bed, and her jaw was set, signifying childish stubbornness. Unwelcome tears sparkled in her eyes. My previous Pilots had thought of similar scenes before, giving me a name for Seiko's imagery. It was a flesh parlor, a common conclusion for a breedling who had otherwise exhausted her purpose.

With a great heave Seiko shoved me out of her head and slammed down her walls. "Screw you, Nanus. Go rot in your cage."

The disconnect was abrupt, like a shower turned on when all the hot water was gone. I shrieked and shook myself, but remembered I was dry in my dark crate, in the garage, quad four of the breedling complex. Until someone deigned to turn on the lights, we would all remain in blackness. Likely no one would turn on the lights—an unnecessary waste of resources on a bankrupt planet.

On my mat I curled up into a ball and reflected on the secrets I had stolen from Seiko. But at what cost? I had hurt my only friend. Without her my place on this planet was nothing but a crumbling empire of dirt.

***

I floated deep underwater while my submersible's hose sucked away at the crevice I had stabbed into the ocean floor with a robotic drill. My impermeable teardrop afforded about as much space as the tunnels I used to dig, but it came with windows. It smelled of mildew sometimes, but never the dead meat odor of bault gas. The ginger stain of silicoat dust had faded from my skin, but I still carried the gems in my pockets.

After the way I assaulted her, Seiko had every right to leave me behind and petition for a new breedling. Instead, I found myself in a position I never dreamed was possible. Seiko's loyalty would have been humbling, if I was capable of such a sentiment.

Seiko and Ahna pressed on my mind the way I imagined my submersible felt the pressure of the ocean straining against its hull—always there, pushing, trying to crumple it into a piece of litter. I had been well behaved, acquiescent, never giving Seiko and Ahna a reason to consider adding reinforcements.

That was all about to change.

"This is a piece of cake," said Ahna. "I could take a nap until Nanus is ready to move to the next strike."

I sensed her relaxation and bunched my muscles as if preparing to deal a physical blow. Ahna was like this lately, unguarded, tranquil—as if she wanted me to take her.

"You think she doesn't wait for that?" said Seiko. "You think Nanus isn't constantly watching for us to relax?"

Ahna laughed, harsh enough to make me flinch. "She's your loyal pet, Seiko. She'll never go anywhere without you."

Seiko was right, though—complacency around me was dangerous. Quickly, before Ahna changed her mind, I launched an assault, piercing her with the sharpest thoughts I could imagine. I envisioned the edges of silicoat glass as I cut through her psyche.

"Stop it!" screamed Seiko. "Nanus, what are you doing?"

I'm a proud little bastard, I thought. *Did you forget?*

"Let her go. *Please.*" Seiko's tears choked her transmission like I imagined them choking in her throat. "Her nose is bleeding."

How close do you sit with her?

"What?" she shrieked.

Is it close enough to touch? Does Ahna ever reach out to you? Take your hand in hers?

Ahna gathered herself for a defensive, but it was weak. My first blow was too brutal.

Has she kissed you, Seiko? Has she shared herself with you?

"You don't know anything about—"

Answer the question!

"Will you let her go? Will you promise to stop hurting her?"

I will, if you're honest with me.

"Then look for yourself." And there she was, Seiko's vital emotions exposed as if her essence was cracked open for surgery.

Ever since Ahna first found Seiko, they had worked side by side, every day, Ahna sitting a hair's breadth away. Seiko had hinted at her feelings on occasion. The few times Seiko worked up the courage to touch her, Ahna turned away under some excuse, so Seiko was never quite sure. Seiko's nights were solitary. The corridors in her poems were real in this place, and she walked them aimlessly, unable to sleep. Her loneliness and uncertainty ate her, drained her, turned her into a shade.

"Now let her go," said Seiko, and she pushed me away.

I eased back on Ahna. Her link went limp and bled away like water down the drain. I waited to see if Seiko would also sever her connection with me. I didn't need Pilots to guide my return to the surface anymore, and Ahna had one thing right—without Seiko there was nowhere I wanted to go.

Later, I didn't know the time, Seiko approached my mind again. "Ahna didn't deserve that. I know you did it on my behalf, but she didn't deserve it. It doesn't make me happy for you to punish someone I love. How will she ever reach out to me if she fears your retribution?"

Ahna would never come to Seiko anyway, regardless of my actions. I had seen it all before Ahna passed out. *Is she okay?* I asked.

"She fell and hit her head," Seiko said. "The concussion was worse than whatever you did to her. It's time you come back to the surface." Seiko mentally fingered our connection as if to pull it loose. "And Nanus, if you do anything like this again, I will end you. No more empty threats. Even if it means they rip out my transmission chips and I never Pilot again."

***

After I secured my submersible for the night, Seiko walked me back to my garage. I hadn't seen her in person in weeks and she had wasted during our time apart.

"I think you need a vacation," I said.

"Sacred Mother's Memoriam of Birth is next week. We'll get a day or two."

"Next week? That means we've been here…" I tried to calculate, but Seiko beat me to it.

"Six months, give or take."

I took Seiko's hand, but she yanked away and retreated several steps. Except in flesh parlors, breedlings and Pilots never touched. It was offensive. Taboo. Not like I cared.

"You've got to stop this," I said. "You're letting this obsession eat you alive."

"You don't know—" said Seiko, but I cut her off.

"I do know. Do you want me to show you what I know?" Through our shared transmission I held up an image of Ahna, pristine like the portraits of hallowed subjects displayed on the holy days. It was Seiko's own idealistic notion of Ahna and I was ready to rip it to shreds, but nothing I had done to Seiko in our life together would compare to the pain of showing her the truth of Ahna's feelings unless Seiko really wanted it—unless she was ready to surrender.

"No!" Seiko shrieked and grabbed me, unaware of herself. Some of the other Pilots passing over the concourse between submersible bay and the dormitories gasped and looked away. Seiko dropped her hands again. "Nanus, no. Whatever you think you know, whatever you think you saw in her head, it's not reality. The things in our thoughts are distorted by imagination and emotion."

I showed Seiko what I uncovered of her feelings for Ahna the day I tore into her defenses back on the planet with the bault mines. "Not real?" I asked.

Seiko covered her face with her hands as if to shut out the vision, but the image wasn't before her eyes and I wouldn't make it go away until she answered me.

"Yes," Seiko said. "For me, it's real."

I projected an image of the little girl I had found, hiding in the same place where Seiko hid her feelings for Ahna. The girl was silicoat stained and hunched from working in a tunnel half her size. How could I force Seiko to choose between real and not real if I wouldn't do it for myself? "Not real?"

"Real," Seiko whispered. "It's real, you little bitch. Don't ever ask me to tell you that again."

***

"Welcome back, Ahna." I sat on the floor of my crate, stumpy legs dangling over the edge. Ahna sat beside me, perched on top of my stepstool. This was the first time I had ever seen her in person and she was older than I expected—streaks of silver shot through her dark hair, fine crinkles lined the skin around her eyes and lips. When Seiko thought of Ahna, she always pictured her as timeless and radiant.

It was so unlike Ahna to visit the breedling quad, to show any concern or awareness of me beyond my role as a tool. Her presence here made me uneasy and I wondered what it meant. Ahna had brought me a cup of beer and a slice of cake in honor of Sacred Mother's Memoriam of Birth; the day we paid homage to the one from whom all breedling life sprang. I pictured the Sacred Mother shaped very much like a test tube, but the prints and holographs hung up in her honor showed her humble headed, sweet smiling, and glowing in soft, gold light. "How's your head?" I asked.

Ahna grimaced. "Still attached to my shoulders, no thanks to you."

"Would you believe me if I said I regretted it?"

"I believe you," she said. "You love Seiko. You would kill for her."

"I wasn't going to kill you," I said. "I just had to know the truth."

"Why haven't you told Seiko what you saw in my head?"

"It would destroy her."

Ahna nodded her agreement. "She doesn't really love me— just some idea of me that she's made up. Why doesn't she find someone else, Nanus? Why is she killing herself over me?"

"She's afraid because it means risking her hope. You've never turned her away, and that's better than taking the risk that someone else might. It's the only thing that keeps her going. The hurt is as real to her as the love, maybe more so. Feeling *something* is what matters to her most."

Ahna lowered her mental defenses enough to let me see how well she understood this.

"Where is Seiko anyway?" I asked.

"Sleeping in, I think. She was up late, roaming the halls."

"You saw her?"

"She knocked on my door."

"She did?" I said.

Ahna nodded. "I pretended no one was home."

***

Seiko showed up with more beer and cake as my first helping ran out. From the way she swayed and stumbled as she made her way across the garage, I knew she had started on the beer long before she came to share any with Ahna and me. Seiko's face, sallow and thin, lit up at the sight of her beloved. "They said I would find you here," she said.

Seiko sank to the floor beside Ahna and she wore her emotions plain on her face. One dip into Seiko's head revealed how she held herself unguarded for anyone to see, inviting Ahna to accept or deny her. Maybe it was the beer, or pressure from me, or plain inevitability that inspired Seiko's uncharacteristic openness. Whatever the cause I sensed disaster was the imminent result. *Such a terrible waste*, I thought as I slipped into the shadows of my crate, watching Ahna and Seiko with my eyes and tuning into our shared transmission to observe them with my mind.

I muffled my connection so they felt alone, but listened to their thoughts like a child with a glass pressed against a wall. In Seiko's opened thoughts I learned she had followed Ahna from job to job for years filled with pain, but also with hope. She wanted to forget the years that came before Ahna, the years after she outgrew tunnel diameter restrictions and succumbed to subsistence in the flesh parlors where she taught herself to be numb, to feel nothing. For a long time Seiko did forget, but hope wasn't enough anymore. Like an addict who develops tolerance for her drug, she needed something stronger from Ahna, if she was to keep going.

Ahna broke the silence first. "I've known how you felt for a long time, Seiko. I thought if I ignored it your feelings would go away. I was afraid to hurt you."

"You saved me," said Seiko. "How is that not love? You took me away from that place, that nightmare."

"I was acting on childish idealism. I had a savior complex. I thought if you had the chance, you could become something more than just a used-up breedling."

"Before you I was superfluous trash. Without you, that's still all I am."

"You can't give up, Seiko…for yourself…for Nanus."

"Why? So I can do to her what you did to me? Lead her on for years with false hope."

I sat up and cleared our line, listening with my consciousness, tuned and sharp.

"It's different for her," said Ahna. "Nanus knows."

Seiko jumped to her feet and shrieked. "She knows what? That I don't love her?"

I cried out in a voice that resonated with Seiko's pain; my brain seethed with her agony.

"Seiko, stop it," Ahna said, calm and deliberate. "It doesn't have to be like this."

"*Liar*," Seiko screeched. Reaching into my crate, Seiko jabbed a hand into my pocket and dragged out one of the silicoat stones she knew I always carried. Before either Ahna or I realized what Seiko was up to, she had jabbed the stone into her flesh and cut open her scalp; she wrenched out the Pilot chips and wires installed at the base of her skull.

Seiko flickered once in my mind and then popped like a soap bubble. Gone. Like our daily disconnect, but so much worse.

"What the hell?" Ahna said. "What are you doing?"

Still clutching her chips, Seiko's fist dripped blood, *plip, plip, plip*, on the floor. "Nothing about this was ever real," Seiko said. "Not even me."

Seiko wobbled, took a step back, and caught herself on another breedling's crate.

Ahna approached Seiko, hand outstretched. "Do you know what I had to go through to get that for you? To get you out of that place and make you a Pilot?"

Seiko flung the gruesome mess of blood and wires at Ahna so that it smacked her chest before slopping to the floor, leaving a red streak down Ahna's shirt. "Before you came along," said Seiko, "I denied the existence of love. But you brought me into this world that insisted it was possible, if I believed, if I tried, if I waited long enough. It is the grandest lie ever perpetuated, and I can't believe I fell for it." Seiko stumbled towards the garage door, gathered herself, and then disappeared around the corner.

Seiko! I cried for her in my thoughts, oblivious to the fact that she could no longer hear it. The place she once occupied inside me had distorted into a frigid abyss.

"I'm so, so sorry, Nanus," said Ahana. She leaned down and peered into my crate. "But consider yourself lucky, little one."

My only reply was a snuffled breath and hiccup of tears.

Ahna squared her shoulders and looked towards the exit. "You already know the truth. You won't waste your life chasing a lie."

I followed Ahna's gaze. Only a few feet beyond the door, the concourse opened upon a universe of ocean. Through Ahna's thoughts I knew it was vast, but at the same time growing smaller as people pushed farther and deeper, desperate to charter the unknown and define the boundless. "It's not a lie," I said. "My love for her is real."

THE MEADOW

DINA LYUBER

Dina Lyuber is a writer living in Calgary, Alberta, Canada. She writes both fiction and non-fiction, and also teaches English as a second language. Dina is currently working on her first novel.

Jaydren's eyeballs felt sticky. He rubbed his left eye, gulped down the dregs of his simulated coffee beverage, and sent his notes to Mr. Kalinski before swiping the screen aside. Leaving work, he projected into his status reader, which also updated his changing location as he stepped into the lift and plummeted into the chaotic, twilit streets below. The commuter traffic was particularly awful at this hour, with thousands of bodies pouring out of the glassy office buildings and pushing their way to the bullet trains, shoulder-to-shoulder, each projecting into their readers or scanning their socials. Jaydren tried to fight his way onto a moving walkway, but the crowd was too dense and he had to trudge along with the other pedestrians. Shouldn't have left at rush hour, he projected. Am total sardine. Land vehicles were only permitted on the megaparkways between cities, and Jaydren lived two minor-municipalities away. There were a handful of hovercrafts in the air highways that wound between the buildings. Their bone-deep vibrations drowned out the noise from the crowd. If Jaydren had been born with better prospects, he could be settling into his own hovercraft right now, but his intelligence was a tad below average, and his health and stamina readings had not been great either.

The sun was almost gone and the city had turned brackish brown, the air smoggy and thick with noise. Vids and text ran along glass facades like giant mechanical worms, streaming from one building to another. Jaydren was jostled and heaved forward: debris on a rolling ocean of bodies. He couldn't see beyond the backs of people's heads, but trusted that the crowd was moving in the right direction.

He made it onto the train and fell into a standing pod, strapping himself inside and choosing his point of arrival on the small screen that hovered at eye-level. The pod shifted to the back of the train while empty pods moved forward towards the influx of passengers. Jayden relaxed and focused on his reader. It would be a long ride to his apartment. He switched on his lenses and his vision became saturated with his home platform. He watched a preview for the next episode of Invasion, and his heartbeat quickened with the sudden action: debris flew past him and gunfire exploded in the distance. Then, in a split-second, he was in bed with MAC and Anorita, the show's main characters, embroiled in a hot huddle of blankets.

"No way," he exhaled into the darkness, and when the preview faded, his body was tense, his fists balled in anticipation. He would watch the full episode at home with the use of his sensory apps and telewear equipment.

Next, he browsed his socials. His current background was The Meadow, an undulating grassy field that stretched into the distance. At home, with the proper apps, he could infuse sensations like wind and sunshine onto his platform, and even taste and smell, but here on the train he just watched the yellow-green grass billow in muffled stillness. The train's metallic hum and periodic stop announcements were only just audible. His Friends' avatars were scattered far across the field, organized into navigable clusters. As he approached a Friend, he could hear their updates and see portals pop up around their heads. He browsed a few portals, but didn't Engage with anyone until he reached Savi.

Sooo tired, she updated. Can't wait to relax with my man MAC. Her current location was a shopping district north of the city. A MoonDrops Diner logo hovered next to her avatar, along with the words Savi is enjoying a MoonDrops signature sandwich. She had tinged her hair aquamarine. Her eyes were very dark blue today, and she had the kitty teeth again. Jayden grinned. The sharp little teeth were oddly sexy. Beside her a portal popped up: Savi has invited you to Engage.

Jaydren accepted. "Long day, babe?" he asked.

"You have no idea." Savi was a Greeter, a step below Jaydren in the professional world. Her intelligence scores were comparable to his own, but her family hadn't the money for a PhD, so she'd only graduated with a Masters in Service.

She told him about her long day, and he made consolatory noises. "Why don't you come over to my place tonight," he offered. "We can watch Invasion together. Have you seen the preview?"

"Are you joking? Of course I've seen it! What is with that bedroom scene, right?" Her avatar's eyes ballooned momentarily to show surprise. "I can come by on the train…" She broke off, and Jaydren waited while she worked something out in the real world. She was back a moment later. "I can't wait to see you. I miss you." She sent him a heart icon. "I miss your body," she added.

Jaydren laughed. "Careful now," he said, "I'm on the train."

"I know." Savi's avatar gave an exaggerated wink. "Come on. Don't you miss me?"

"Yeah," breathed Jaydren, "I definitely do."

"Tell me how much you miss me." Her icon puffed the words seductively, and Jaydren pictured the feel of those little teeth on his chest, the hot wetness of her lips. He needed to invest in better sensory apps for his Portable, but they were so expensive.

"Come on, tell me," she insisted.

"You want me to tell you here?" he asked, though he already knew the answer. Savi had a thing for dirty talk in public places. They had connected randomly through a Friend and had sexted virtually a number of times before they'd actually met in person a few months ago.

"Come on, Jaydren, what do you want to do tonight?" she prompted.

Jaydren was caught up in a convoluted description when his pod suddenly jerked to the front of the train and the doors wooshed open. He cut off mid-sentence and stumbled onto the platform, the lenses depixelating until the world came into focus.

He blinked several times, his face hot. Shuffled forward by the crowd behind, he stepped off the platform and onto the walkway home, which was less crowded out here. The buildings here were all residential cement blocks that stood in uniform rows. Jaydren's apartment was a studio, perfectly square apart from the toilet/shower nook at the back. The far wall was a pixelated screen that shone to life when he walked in. On the right-hand side, there was a kitchen counter with a sink and a small cooker. There was an armchair pushed to the side of the room where he usually ate his meals. Most of the room was taken up by his Murphy bed, which Jaydren didn't bother to hide away most mornings since he would just pull it down again when he got home.

He rummaged in his cupboard for a box of Low-carb Noodle Nuggets and shook them into a bowl. He added some water from the tap, and thrust them into the cooker. He found a bottle of simulated wine beverage which he placed on the counter with two glasses. He browsed his socials while he ate, but Savi's avatar was unresponsive. She was probably Engaging with another Friend, or maybe speaking to someone on the train. He Engaged with a few people he knew loosely and watched some media recommended by his reader. Outside his window, the day had turned the bruised colour of night and he could hear the wind picking up outside and whistling through the spaces between the tall buildings.

Savi showed up an hour later. The first three trains had all been full, so she'd waited for almost twenty minutes before finding an empty pod. She stood in the doorway clutching her purse until Jaydren ushered her inside. Savi's real hair was a dull bluish colour with dark-brown roots. She had put in a set of false kitty teeth, and she was still wearing her yellow work uniform beneath her black sweater.

"Come sit on the bed," he said. "I've got some wine. I've got some snacks too, if you're hungry."

"No thanks," Savi said softly, and Jaydren remembered that she'd been eating a sandwich when they'd Engaged. He climbed onto the bed next to her. It was always awkward in those first moments of real-life contact. To fill the silence, he told her a little about his day at work, and she nodded in her quiet way. His apartment was warm, so she took off her sweater and threw it on his armchair. She accepted a glass of wine and took a deep gulp of the purplish liquid. Jaydren leaned against her on the bed. Her bare arms were paunchy and pale from days spent working indoors. He sipped his wine, thinking about his own appearance and how loosely it matched the avatar that Savi had recently Engaged with. He had a long sallow face pockmarked with acne scars. His ginger hair was overdue for a haircut and an itchy stubble stained his upper lip.

Jaydren stood up and dimmed the lights in his apartment. "Let's watch Invasion," he suggested. He finished his wine and poured them both another glass. He also found a bag of Crunchies which they consumed while the episode unfolded around them, the air growing thick with smoke as Anorita's hovercraft hummed down the landscape.

The episode ended with an explosion of credits, and silence filled the room as Jaydren swept away the telewear. "Wow," he whispered.

"I loved it," said Savi. "I can't believe she saved him. I've been waiting for that to happen ever since they met, since that very first day—"

"When MAC found her hiding-out in the pit of his space station? Yeah, me too. And the chase scene—"

"That was epic. That was absolutely amazing." Savi inhaled deeply, her round face exalted in the shadows of his bedroom. "I'm going to remember this episode for the rest of my life."

"I know!" Jaydren's body thrummed with the recent adrenaline rush. His arm was still against Savi's, and the image of MAC and Anorita in bed together, their muscular bodies writhing against each other, was still warm in his mind. He brushed away the near-empty Crunchies bag and gently took her wine glass to the counter. When he sat back down on the bed, he kissed her tentatively on her salty mouth, tasting of Crunchies' seasoning. She kissed him back, her lips moving wetly against his. He began to peel off her clothes, and in the dimness her hands found his belt buckle. They didn't speak, but both were breathing noisily as Jaydren rolled on top of her. He closed his eyes and saw Anorita's tumbling black hair and her large, cinnamon-coloured breasts, her body arching beneath MAC's and her muscular legs wrapping around his torso.

Breathing hard, he rolled off Savi. She was sweaty and warm beside him. Jaydren closed his eyes. He drifted near sleep. At some point, he felt Savi sit up and feel around for her clothing. When he opened his eyes, she was pulling on her shoes. "This was fun," she said.

"Yeah," Jaydren agreed thickly. "You should stay," he added, though in truth he didn't much care either way. He was pulled heavily back towards sleep.

"No, I can't, but thanks for the offer." She picked up her sweater from his armchair.

"Ok. Let's get together later."

"Ok," said Savi. She brushed her bluish hair back. Jaydren noticed she had taken out her kitty teeth. "I'll catch you on my reader," she said.

She left, and Jaydren rolled back against the pillows, pulling his crumpled blankets to his chin. He could hear the wind again, whistling between the buildings. Somewhere in the depths of sleep, he found himself walking through The Meadow. There were no avatars in the tall, swaying grass. He walked aimlessly beneath a static sky, searching for Anorita, but the meadow was wide and empty, and the wind gusted through it all night long.

WHAT THE WORLD TAKES

MELISSA SCHNARR-RICE

Melissa is a writer, game designer and semi-professional nerd. She lives in London, Ontario, but don't hold it against her.

The dream always comes before a storm hits. I know it by heart—even my dreamself knows what's going to happen next. The great bear twists her head towards us and in her eyes, it's clear—she's turned. Behind me, Alex and Mark curse and run. The bear roars. It is thunder, breaking clouds. It rattles through me, icy hot fear flashes up my spine and claws at the back of my skull. Time slows. My grandfather, my mishomis' voice pierces the thick veil that's muffling my senses. *Never run from a predator—never become prey. Running just makes them want you more.* For a sliver of second, I'm angry—that's the only thing my brain offers up when faced with a bear?

She is slow as she begins her lunge towards me. The world is slow and my brain takes in every detail—her dark fur bristling, the slick of her black nose, the vapour of her breath as it splits the morning mist. I hear her grunts; they clatter and bounce inside my gut. Time speeds up just as she does. My blood beats through me with each thump of her paws, as they hit and tear at the earth. For a few seconds, this rhythm connects us. The ground is shaking, or is it me? My grandfather's words hold me where I am. Fear holds me where I am.

Then the gun is in my hand. It points at her.

Bear charged me once. I shot it straight in the head. Didn't even faze it. Their skull's so thick, the bullet ricocheted and killed my dog instead. Mishomis's voice, his story about the bear. My finger pulls the trigger and I wonder if this bullet will kill me instead.

Somehow, it doesn't.

Somehow, it rips through her eye. She dies instantly. Her head and front dip and crash into the ground, breaking her thunderous stride. She slides and tumbles through the grass.

The great bear is dead at my feet when Alex and Mark return. Later they'll tell me that the gunshot made them stop their flight while the silence afterward brought them back. The gun is still in my hand and Alex has to pry it from my fingers. The great bear's body is steaming in the morning chill. Her meat is poison. All I can think is, *did I waste a bullet?* Maybe I say it because Alex hugs me and Mark laughs. I wonder how many great bears are left.

That's when we hear her baby cry.

"Sis, sis!" *No. It doesn't say that …*

"Sis, they want you."

I open my eyes slowly. Grey darkness greets me. I can tell from the dizziness swimming in my head—even as I push into the waking world—that I haven't slept for more than an hour. Seth is standing in the doorway, the door cracked just enough so that he can poke his head in.

"Sis?"

"I'm…awake," I admit reluctantly. I sit up and rub my eyes, trying to ward away the nausea of waking too early, sleeping too little. The chill in the air sobers me a bit. Enough light escapes the hallway for me to make out the sheepish look on my little brother's face. "It's okay, Seth. I'm not mad."

"They always send me when you're trying to get some rest," he says. "I'm sorry."

I stand up and stretch. Seth picks up my boots by the door and tosses them over to me. The world outside has painted my windows black. The dead of night creeps by so slowly lately.

"What's this about?" I realize that my breath is coming out as small puffs when I speak. Briefly, I consider wrapping a blanket around me, *no that won't do. I have to look—formidable.*

"You know they never tell me anything," Seth says as I pull on my boots.

I manage the walk over to my brother without feeling dizzy.

"I don't think it's good," Seth admits as we walk together down the hallway. He fidgets with his hair, tucking it behind his ears.

Sometimes when we walk like this, the building melts away. Seth is a full head taller than me, lanky but strong. There was a time though, when he would not go anywhere unless he was holding my hand. We walked for days, hand-in-hand, until our palms were raw.

The floor creaks and cracks as we make our way. There are holes to watch out for, but the candles along the walls do a good job of lighting the corridor. This hotel is a ruin like any structure that survived, standing tall, stubborn, but deteriorating on the inside. Morgan wants us to leave, find somewhere new where we can make our own shelters. He's never had to tread the snows before, with nothing to eat but frozen grass and your own clothes. He does not know how hungry the world gets.

Seth pulls a candle from a sconce as we hit the end of the hallway where the floor splits into staircases going up and down. He leads the descent, the light of the candle barely pushing away the shadows.

I was afraid of that darkness once. At the time, I had never known true darkness—the cities were all full of lights that did not burn out, candles that buzzed and hummed. They were campfires, so bright they washed out the stars.

I remember the bloom of the city against the black as we drove away that first night in the darkness. The pitch clawed at the windows of the car. The only light came from the dash, casting my mother's face in a sickly green glow.

"Where are we going, Momma?"

"Somewhere safe."

The dirt road bucked our car and Seth, in the back, woke up and began to cry. He was only five then. *He's scared*, I knew. I took off my seatbelt and climbed into the backseat beside him. Seth had a fistful of his favourite blankie as he wailed. I wrapped my arms around him like Momma showed me, so that he couldn't hurt himself or me.

I could see my mother smiling in the mirror above her head. "That's it, sweetie. Look after your brother. You keep him calm."

In my mind, I see her smiling perfectly without the green glow. The thing that happens next—the look she makes—I keep in my own darkness and never bring a candle to it.

Seth and I reach the ground floor. Damien is waiting for me.

"Thanks, Seth," Damien says. He's holding a small lantern that casts tendrils of light across his face.

Seth nods but looks away. He does not look at people's faces. He did not look at me until he was five.

"I'm sorry. This couldn't wait," Damien says. Damien is older than me but he remembers less about Before than I do. He told me once that he wrapped his childhood around a rock and threw it into a lake. *It's better to look ahead*, he had said. *I've seen too many of us get lost in the past.*

Part of me knows that I should be nervous. Even half obscured by the dark, the disquiet in his face is clear; his eyes tell me that something has shaken him.

"Whatever it is, it'll be okay," I tell him. That mantra Seth and I used to share with each other. Say it with confidence and people will believe it.

Damien nods. "We should…go," he says, looking to Seth and then to me.

In silence, we part ways. Seth blows out the candle he's been keeping for my benefit and disappears into the shadows of the stairwell as Damien and I begin walking together. The only sounds are our feet, the crackle of the lantern's flame and the clink of the revolver at my waist.

The ground floor had been hollowed out by some group before us. It is just empty space with wide pillars at regular intervals and metal barrels we hold the fires in. The only exception is the tiny room tucked into a corner—where a door with the word "Maintenance" stands, sentinel against the emptiness.

Damien turns the knob to the door, holding the lantern in front of him as I follow. The hole in the floor, dug out and adorned with makeshift, wooden steps, is just big enough for one person to fit through at a time. The firelight from down below makes the little room glow. Damien blows out the lantern and heads down the stairs.

The proper stairwell to the building's basement had caved in shortly after we found the place. Mark had taken a pickaxe to the floor to reclaim the under levels; *we cannot let the world take back everything*, he had said. *We need a cellar for our cabbages.*

Torches light the corridors, one for every few steps, giving off just enough firelight to see but maintaining just enough shadow to always remind us that here we traverse the intestines of the earth. We pass the room called "Boiler", the council room.

"I've spoken to Fariq and Padma already," Damien says. "Manu is on a hunt tonight—well, I guess you know that." He stops in the middle of the hallway; his gaze sets on the door at the end of the corridor. He does not say anything for long moments.

"Tell me."

His lips move once before the words come out. "They found him. Corso came across his tracks on the hunt—"

"Is Corso alright?" The words spill out, trying to buttress the bloody images in my head.

"No worse for the wear." Damien steps to the side and I notice the figure standing by the door at the end. Corso gives a little salute. *Why is he guarding the do*—then I realize.

"He's in there, isn't he?"

Damien gives a painful nod. "He is. They brought him back." He turns to the door at the end of the hallway again. "It's been decided that it's best if we deal with this tonight."

Though I know by *we*, he means me.

I hear my voice tell him, "I understand," and I'm moving, but really I'm falling into a moment that feels so long ago, a hole in the ground...

The jaws of the bear trap crunch against my leg with such a force, such pain that—for an instant—I *know* my foot's been severed. I scream so loud it hurts, like fingernails tearing at the inside of my throat. I barely feel the wet ground as I crash down into it.

Seth is two strides ahead of me. He is somewhere around twelve years old, no longer a boy but not yet a man. The face he makes when he looks back scares me—I don't want to look. The pain is so intense, the world becomes too bright to bear. I can feel the blood rushing through the veins at my temples—my ankle is nothing but white, hot light...

I think I pass out. When I open my eyes again, Seth is hovering over me, his mouth opening and closing with no words coming out. I want to tell him that it's okay, but all I can manage is another scream. Then, "Go!" *Run. Keep running.*

He doesn't.

His hands are like ice around my leg.

"Blood," Seth says. "You're bleeding."

I try to answer but I scream again. I bite my tongue and taste rust.

Somewhere, in the back of my mind, I'm standing paces away, watching this whole thing as it unfolds. I'm twisted on the ground. Seth is kneeling over me, trying to wrap his hands around my leg where the bear trap holds me, trying to stop the bleeding.

There's voices and movement in the distance, rustling leaves and wet muck sounds. I need to get Seth to move. *They're going to get him.*

But I'm crying in the mud.

My feet splash through half-frozen puddles as we walk down the remainder of the underground corridor. Damien is behind me. He hasn't said anything. There's not much to say.

The torches float by.

Corso is standing guard outside the final door. The letters on this one have long since fallen off—this is the room that has no name.

"He's tied up to one of them pipes," Corso tells me as I near the door. There are a few scratches on his face, but in the shadows they seem to blend in with his other scars.

My hand grabs for the knob and turns it in one fluid motion. The door opens and I move with it, like a gust of wind. I'm in. I'm standing before him. The revolver is in my hand. I point it at his head—

His head is bloodied, hair caked with mud. He is shriveled like a corn husk. The tips of his fingers are black from frostbite.

I must kill him.

I point the gun at his head.

I draw back the hammer.

This is not the first man that I have shot, but I pray it will be the last.

I must kill him.

My heart is beating against my insides, pumping blood so hard my fingers can't seem to hold the gun. *Why did they bring him back?* I must kill him—my finger wraps around the trigger. I *must* kill him—

I can't.

***

The world beyond my eyelids is too bright. I know, even before I open them, that it has snowed again—that the sky is cloudless and that the sun is dancing across the white surface everywhere. Manu is beside me. He must have returned from his hunt sometime in the night. I should be cold, but his arm is wrapped around me. I can tell by the way he's breathing that he's sleeping deeply. I must have been sleeping deeply. I don't remember making it back to bed, let alone his return. One benefit of sleeping too little is that sleep always comes quickly, even when it shouldn't.

It's easy to stay like this—groggy and warm. I could sink into the soft rhythm of his breath against the back of my neck… Last night feels like a fever dream I sweated out.

The revolver is on the table beside the bed.

Sometimes I forget to take it off when I lay down. Manu hates that. The grip jabs him in the gut. He says one of us will get shot. He's never used a gun. He doesn't know how they work.

So, you're the one who slew the bear, was the first thing he said to me. I had never heard anyone speak like that before. The sounds of his words were foreign, yet familiar. I remember blushing and looking at the black swirls that covered his shoulder.

He took a fish from the pile, laid it out across a rock and took a knife from his pocket.

"Who taught you how to cut fish?" He slit the fish's cheek.

"My grandfather."

He smiled. "My grandfather, too."

Manu groans a little as I move his hand and slowly sit up. The sitting up clears my head. I swing my legs around the edge of the bed, stretch out my toes. The brightness in the room tears at my eyes but they adjust as they always do. That is our curse—that our bodies adapt to the world around them, even when our minds do not.

Is killing a monster a waste of a bullet? Misho told me not to waste them.

Manu grabs me by the elbow lightly. "Go to sleep."

He never speaks of his home, though I know he dreams about it. I picture a village by the ocean, full of dark-skinned, dark-eyed people that talk like him, people with black swirl markings on their bodies.

"How do you say hello where you come from?" I asked one day as we cleaned fish.

He didn't respond. I thought I had offended him. There were many people that did not like to talk about Before. I decided not to push.

"Do you know who Nanabozho is?"

He shook his head.

"He was a trickster and a shapeshifter. He could change into anything he wanted. People would say 'boozhoo' to each other when they met. Like 'hello', but they were really asking if the other person was Nanabozho playing a trick."

He laughed.

I looked at him. "Boozhoo," I said.

"Kia ora," he said.

The silence in the room unsettles both of us. I can't think of what to say—why I can't go back to sleep. What is tied up in the basement…I cannot say the words. Manu sits up behind me.

"I know," is all he says.

"Do you? Because I don't. They were supposed to bring back food. They brought that thing instead…" The words are sharp rocks that fall out of my mouth, cutting my tongue and lips. "I know what they *expect* me to do, what I should do. But I couldn't. I—couldn't."

Manu wraps his hand around mine and only then do I realize it's shaking. I stand up, cross over to the window. The cold seeping in from outside is a welcome distraction, a pause in the landslide. *Maybe if I stand here long enough the words will freeze.* Winter's been so long this year, I wonder if the sun remembers what grass looks like.

This is the world. The little town that once lived here is mostly flat with only a few structures jutting out of the snow. The cedars in the distance are the only break in white. Sometimes, when I look out this window, I think I see a great bear moving through the trees. I like to pretend that this is the bear I chose not to shoot, the cub screaming in the woods that Seth and I took in. We called her Moon; she followed us from camp to camp until one spring when she did not return.

My arms are crossed against my chest, whether this is defense against the cold or further conversation, I can't really say. Maybe it's both. Probably it's both. Manu is sitting with his arms resting on his knees.

"You know the council will agree to whatever you think is best," he says after a moment.

"Why? I've never understood why." Anger now, I feel it in my gut. It seems unfair to be angry at him but I'm angry all the same.

Manu shrugs. His silence makes me angrier. Then he turns to me:

"You remember the army camp? Fort Leve I think they called it. Padma and her group set us on that path when they joined us. We left the woods, trudged through that bog…I didn't think it was possible, but the more they talked about it, the closer we got…I started to hope that it was all true. We'd get there and there would be people, *houses with people* and medicine and food. I hoped for that.

"Then we found it and it was…just ashes and bones. A huge fence protecting a few ripped tents." He looks away now, looks at his hands. "I wanted to die that day. That was the day I realized that it really was all gone—and that we were never getting it back." Silence again. After a moment, he laughs. "But then you and Seth started clearing a space underneath one of those big tents, for a fire."

What are you doing? Alex had asked me. The question made me stop and look around. Mark was kneeling in the mud near the entrance to the camp. I remember the hollowness in everyone's faces. But it had been raining. Seth had told me that he was cold.

"We needed to dry off," I say. It seemed so simple at the time.

"Yeah, well, we needed that."

I leave him to sleep.

The hallway is empty, though most of the doors along its sides are open. I can hear movement. People downstairs. Most of them are awake by now. I can see the activity on the ground floor as if I were standing there in the middle of it. People building fires, keeping fires, boiling water for cooking and cleaning. Others tending the goats and sheep that we keep in the remnants of the building next door. Others still, in pairs, patrolling this place we call ours.

Last night's nausea returns.

I make my way down the hallway, stopping at the stairs.

The cat we call Boo is sitting on the first step leading up. He is all white and hard to see when he bounces in the snow. Today he is holding a little brown mouse in his teeth.

When he sees me, he drops the mouse and meows. I sit down beside him, giving in. He purrs as I pet him.

Kitty was the first word Seth ever said. It was the name he gave the plush tiger our mother bought him for his third birthday. Mum handed it to him with a big red bow around its neck and he clapped and said *Kitty! Kitty!* There were tears in my mother's eyes. At the time, I didn't understand why that made her cry.

Seth didn't really speak until he was almost seven. For the longest time, he called me 'sweetie', because that's what Mum always called me. He said 'no' and 'this' and 'sweetie' but not much else, and then one day sat down beside Misho and told him all about the radishes we were growing in the little garden outside the cabin.

Somedays, I wish we never left the cabin.

I don't know how long we were in the woods by ourselves. When I think back to the night we left the city, what things my mother put into the trunk of the blue car, the roads we took…I think we were heading to my grandfather's—my mishomis's was that *somewhere safe.*

I grabbed the pup tent, the bag of food and the backpack Mum had packed for me from out of the trunk before the car sank completely into the ditch full of bullrush. Seth stood on the side of the road with his blankie and Kitty. He wasn't crying anymore. I decided that meant I couldn't cry either.

At first, I pretended it was like any summer at our grandfather's—I told Seth that Momma and Mishomis were coming. I lied to him every day. I made a game of it for as long as I could. We followed a river, stuck to the trees. We made a camp at night and I made a fire using a flint striker and birch bark just like Mishomis had showed me a hundred times before. We walked during the day in the bush, like when Mishomis took me out along the traplines. I told Seth that we were trappers now. He said *traptraptap* sometimes and it always made me laugh.

When we found the cabin, I thought it was abandoned. The door was not locked. The wind opened it and closed it as we neared. Inside, it looked as though someone had come in and torn everything off the shelves. Seth let go of my hand and went running after a can of beans that was rolling on the ground. It was empty.

"This," he said, throwing the can away.

I walked around the place. It was one big room. There was a black metal stove in one corner, a sink and counter. One wall was entirely a bookshelf. There was a pile of furniture off to the far right and maybe a bed behind it, I couldn't see. Seth ran towards the back door, as another gust of wind blew it open.

"Seth!" I called after him as he disappeared behind the stack of furniture.

"Sweetie?" he said.

I rounded the pile of furniture. There was a bed, and laying on it, an old man. I thought the old man was dead and I grabbed for Seth, wanting to keep him away. Seth dodged me, clumsily falling into the edge of the bed. When I helped him up, I realized that the old man's mouth was moving, just barely; his lips were so dry and cracked, no sound could escape.

"Misho," Seth said.

He knew that wasn't *our* mishomis but he didn't care. He opened the bag I had him carrying and brought out his water bottle.

"This," he said as he walked over and placed the bottle on the table beside the bed.

Boo gets tired of chin scratches and returns to his mouse. My stomach turns as he begins to pull at the head.

I find myself wandering upwards. Past the fourth floor, where everyone sleeps, there are candle stubs sitting in clusters every two or three steps. This is my unkept secret. A self-imposed exile I adopt sometimes.

The roof, eight storeys off the ground, is bitter in the winter wind. No one comes up here but me. There is an old armchair with a tarp over it left over from the last group who passed through. I imagine whoever sat up here was their watchman, though what he or she was watching for I couldn't say. The fires did not reach this far and as for other groups…I've seen more bones than people, more graves than footprints. I do not look for people when I sit here.

I grab a blanket hanging by a hook before stepping out into cold sunlight. The seat of the armchair has a dusting of snow that's easily wiped off. There is a metal drum meant for a fire beside the chair. I feel like, with a fire crackling beside me, I could nap here undisturbed. I've never lit a fire because of that.

As I settle into the armchair, bundle into the thick blanket, I take off the revolver. It is shiny silver—a single action. Single action means you have to pull the hammer back each time you shoot, you have to think about every shot. I swing out the cylinder and spin it with a finger. This is a habit. There are two rounds, and two spent. When the cylinder spins, the bullets and empty spaces blur together making it seem both full and empty at the same time.

There are lots of guns still, Mark had said when I showed it to him, *but not so many bullets left.*

He saved my life and my leg. He found us in the mud, Seth and I, pried me from the bear trap, took us in.

"You're lucky." His hands were red with blood, my blood, when I woke up in the camp.

"Lucky?" My voice did not sound like me. The pain throbbed in place of searing. There were bandages around my leg.

"That trap snatched you at the sides." He made a bear trap with his hands. "The other way, and the bone would have snapped."

I drifted in and out, hearing voices through half-dreams. Sometimes Seth would talk to me. I don't know if I answered. Another time, I woke—Seth was snoring somewhere close; Mark was sitting near the entrance to the tent.

"Why did you run away from us?" he asked.

"I don't know. I was afraid," I said.

"Of us?"

"People," I said.

"Yeah." Mark nodded. "People can be dangerous."

I could not walk for days and days, so I read his books instead. Mark knew all about the world Before. He scavenged for knowledge instead of food, brought back books and maps and little things. *This is a sparkplug. This is a thumb drive. This is a corkscrew. This is a beer stein.*

I hear the door to the roof screech open and Seth appears. He crosses the distance between us with a cup in each hand.

"They're looking for you. Well, they know where you are. So. I guess they're waiting for you." He sets a mug full of steaming dark liquid into my hands. "Padma told me to come up here and give you this." He sits down on a crate I often use as a footrest.

I can smell the cranberry, the wild rose, the bitter chicory in the tea as its steam wafts upwards. I take a sip of the sweet-then-bitter drink before asking the inevitable question. "What do they want?"

Seth shrugs. "Damien said to Padma that they need to take some people off of woodcutting and fires to cut the meat that Manu and the other hunters brought in. Padma said we're too low on wood and that the hunters can do it once they have some sleep. Morgan said that he saw a bird and it means winter is over so we should start preparing to leave. Lots of people are wondering where Corso is..." He looks at me and stops. There is probably more—this is always more, but he turns to the mug in his hands and begins to drink instead.

"Corso's downstairs," but that is not the full answer. Half-truths are for the others. The words I have to say are staring me in the face, the way the dogs stare one another down. I force myself to look. "Mark is downstairs."

"Corso is guarding him," Seth concludes. His response is immediate, matter of fact. He takes another sip.

I'd like to stay in this moment, as simple and banal as it is. Seth could tell me all the rest—how the washers are wanting to redraw jobs for the week, how we're low on willow bark, how we ought to clean up the other floors, fortify them, how we ought to leave again...

But I've said the words, made it real. They are a choker around my throat. The room without a name tugs.

"You have to kill him," Seth says.

"Yeah...I do."

He nods and takes a pinch of snow from the ledge of the roof and drops it into his cup. *You can't die of thirst in the winter,* he told me once.

"I have to kill Mark." The words come out quietly but they are crisp and clean. In the cold sun, in front of Seth, this is a truth

I cannot ignore. This is the world, we cannot hide from it.

Seth shakes his head. "His name is not Mark," he says. "His name is Wendigo."

"I have to go," I tell my little brother. The standing up is not as hard as saying the words; things begin to tumble now, on their own course. "The hunters can sleep all day if they want. Let everyone know that. The washers will look after the meat today. Tell Morgan that we're not going anywhere and tell Padma that we'll need more people on woodcutting. We'll need enough for a pyre."

***

He is no longer sitting by the pipes. The twine that bound him there now hangs, frayed and chewed. He is lying in the middle of the floor. If his eyes still see, they are focused on the lantern that hangs above, too high out of reach. The lantern's candle is low, barely casting any light over the sides.

His lips are moving. I cannot hear what he is saying, but I know the words.

"This is the world. This is the world. This is the world." His mantra, like a ladder of words.

The revolver is in my hand.

He looks. From where he lays, his head jerks to the side and back. The whites of his eyes are bloodshot.

When we found him, he was never still. His eyes wandered. His fingers danced. We thought that he and Alex and the others had been lost in the blizzard.

I remember holding the little stick in my hand, died red with cranberries the day we drew those lots. Red for hunters. "You're not much of a hunter. We should redraw the assignments."

"No. This is the system that the group's agreed to," Mark

said. "I may not be the greatest huntsman, but I can help with the gear, carry any kills, tend the fires."

The hunting party, four in all, went out into the white. It's easier to think that none of them returned.

I expect him to say something; I want him to say something, something to replace the memory of his bloody hands, the smell of burnt hair, the bones—the indignant way he said, *I had to eat. I needed the meat.* So matter of fact, it made Damien throw up.

This is the world, this is the world, this is the world …

In my dream, I remember the voice of the bear, her thunder, but never the blast of the gun.

Light explodes from it and fills the room, shattering the darkness for an instant. The sound is the crack of a great cedar falling, shaking me as it hits the earth. It is the sound of the world taking back one last thing from Before. It is a bear's roar.

BITS & PIECES
TINA SHELTON

Tina's career includes a published novel titled "*The Corsican*", a trunk novel with more revisions than a hydra has heads, and a promising, soon to be published novel called "*Bento Box*". She also has two published short stories, "*The Gaijin and the Butterfly*" and "*Bits & Pieces.*" She's bootstrapped her way up from a novice to her current position with a lot of hard work and fun, and loves telling stories more than anything. She's married and has a son, who are her most avid (and critical!) audience.

The Five Sisters were more than five, and they weren't necessarily sisters, but they were all women, and they were more terrifying than the four male societies combined. These ladies were small, dusky-skinned women, comfortable with a bow, an M-16, or a Farcry rocket launcher. They believed in defending their people, in any way they could.

Heelee was one such lady. Born of the Apsaalooka tribe, Heelee felt it was her destiny to be one of the Chiaxxa Bia, the Five Sisters. The youngest of five, the elder four all brothers, Heelee punched and kicked and bit her way into being a respected fighter. When the council elders deemed her fit for the Trials, she was the youngest Apsaalooka to attempt it in living memory.

Some whispered that Heelee was cursed; she excelled in the baaschiili weapons, the forbidden technology. There were those who felt that anyone that good at the weapons of the technological people should not be living among the simple folk of the NaN, where such items were condemned.

Heelee did not feel cursed. She felt blessed to be called upon to defend her people. If she were truly cursed, then she hoped that dying in defense of her people would end the curse and free her spirit. She took it as a sign when she was accepted by the Chiaaxa Bia that things were as they were meant to be, and she lived her life, accepted by her sisters, hated by her brothers, and feared by her people.

The lands of the NaN were couched between the Republic

to the east, the Confed to the south, and the Coastal lands to the west. To the north lay the land of Canada, but the border was a solid wall of concrete and steel, and no one went in or out. It was a poorly kept secret that tech smugglers, looking to avoid the Confed's tariffs, took the high road and snuck through NaN territory. This was a dangerous proposal. While the smugglers had a lot of land to hide in, the NaN peoples were secretive, distrustful of strangers, and comfortable killing. They didn't have GPS but they did have trackers who could follow the flight of a feather's path three days after it flew.

The warriors had one directive: to keep the lands free of unwelcome guests. Bands of Mountain Teeth, Painted Dogs, and Silent Strangers roamed the plains and badlands. The warriors kept to a strict code. They were never to kill another warrior for any reason. The warriors were highly competitive between their sects and often times looked for ways to outperform each other in combat. Every sect had its specialty. However, if a threat loomed, all problems were set aside in favor of destroying their enemies. The rules were clear, and effective.

The Painted Dogs were a group of jesters, who followed Coyote and harried their prey with taunts as well as spears. The Mountain Teeth were strong, a united front of relentless warriors that would stand together as a mountain range might, defending the land. The Silent Strangers preferred to quietly sneak up on their enemies, giving them no warning. The Hellhounds accepted men who were not from the Tribes. They excelled at using technology, and were widely avoided by the other societies.

The Chiaxxa Bia were another matter entirely. They were not one of the original warrior sects. In fact, they replaced the Feather Scouts, who had died to a man in a shootout years past. The first Chiaxxa Bia were in fact five sisters, daughters of the last standing Feather Scout. They took up his mantle, but not his specialty. It is believed that was the cause of the rift between them, but in truth it was because they were women warriors, who raised themselves up without permission of the elders.

The Chiaxxa Bia survived, thrived, and now stood as large as any of the other men's warrior castes. They were also a thorn in the sides of those castes. The friendly competition between the castes grew more fierce when a Chiaxxa Bia was involved. Pride grew more brittle. Tempers flared. Despite the year being 2294, the people of the NaN did not see women as being equal when it came to being warriors. The Chiaxxa Bia begged to differ.

It was usual, then, for a group of Chiaxxa Bia out on patrol, to be the only caste around. Which was just as Heelee liked it. She learned the ways of the other castes, and decided they were all fools. Riding with her band, Challa, Prexxi, Danya and Fonn, she was the happiest she'd ever been. She wore her talisman against evil, a small stone worn flat on one side and raised on the other. Everyone in the group wore leathers, tanned and sewn by an Elder Chiaxxa Bia, Wind's Melody. She was a winter apple of a woman, brown and wrinkled with a round figure, but none crossed her. She could hunt, kill, clean, and cook any animal on land, and liked to threaten young Chiaxxa with being thrown in a soup pot.

The day was cold, but clear; the sky, blue and cloudless. The women rode horses. Heelee's horse, Hop, was a burly young buckskin. She called him Hop because of his tendency to spook at shadows. Two of the women played a game with knives, testing each other's skills. Another one rode up ahead, keeping an eye out on the horizon.

"You're quiet today, Heelee." Fonn appeared at her elbow, riding Nightdrops, her Appaloosa. "Is something bothering you?"

Heelee looked at her bandmate. Fonn was tall, almost as tall as a man, and she wore her hair in a single thick braid down her back. She had a fondness for colored stones, and wore turquoise, amethyst, and rose quartz in profusion down the sleeves of her shirt. She was a great shot, and very fast when she ran.

"It's been days." Heelee sighed. "I grow restless."

Fonn nodded in understanding. She loved battle, too. "It's good that it's been days, Heelee. It means that we are keeping our people safe."

"I agree, but that does nothing for me when the road is long and everyone smells like tanning leather." Heelee made a face.

Fonn laughed. "There are ways to make the evenings more agreeable."

"There is. Violence." Heelee deliberately steered the conversation away from Fonn's obvious attempt. Heelee liked Fonn, but relationships between two warriors made things complicated. Heelee wanted a less competitive mate.

Her bandmate laughed and let it go, unperturbed by Heelee's redirection. "You are invited, if you choose. I will leave you, as you wish."

The day continued on until Heelee felt the back of her eyes prickle, as they did when twilight crept in. Deer emerged from their beds in the high grass, unconcerned by the horses and the humans. The dimming daylight brought them to a halt. Heelee dismounted from Hop and grabbed the carcass of the rabbit she found an hour or so ago. She took Hop's halter off and let him loose to graze. Then she walked some paces away and made quick work of cleaning her contribution to dinner.

After food, the women sat around a small fire, from a cleared-out, stone-lined pit Fonn built just for the purpose. Danya told a story, entertaining the small band. "The Mountain Teeth stood proudly, side by side, creating a blockade with their bodies. They began their chant of strength, luring their enemy out. Trillia did not make a sound, but laughed on the inside. Her sisters were free to leave the trap, and left no trace of themselves behind."

The band laughed at the cleverness of Trillia, and how she tricked the proud Mountain Teeth. As they laughed, Heelee thought she heard something more sinister. She shushed her sisters with a hand gesture, and then got up and started towards the noise. By then they could all hear it. Something with an engine growled on its way past.

The women whistled for their horses, and mounted swiftly. Bows, arrows, guns, and knives blossomed in the twilight like spiky desert plants. They rode towards the sound, which sounded nearer.

In the swiftly darkening evening, a rumbling sort of monster trolled its way through the tall prairie grass. It belched noxious fumes and made horrible sounds. The conveyance was square, with some kind of reinforced wheels to traverse the uneven, treacherous ground. There were several names for what the Apsaalooka people called them, each more colorful than the last. The Chiaxxa Bia called them stinkwagons.

This stinkwagon was a black box with little slits for allowing air circulation. A turret appeared populated by a single man. The methodical way that he swung the large gun back and forth suggested he searched for targets. When the Chiaxxa Bia became visible, riding towards the stinkwagon, he raised the cry. Then he took aim.

The Chiaxxa Bia scattered when the bullets rained down upon them. Puffs of dust coiled up to show where the bullets impacted the ground. Heelee could hear shouts from within the stinkwagon. More guns coughed, the deep sounds loud in the night. Stars began peeking out from behind a black curtain of clouds, as though cautiously interested.

Heelee saw Fonn's Appaloosa running without a rider, and her breath caught. She looked at the stinkwagon, and saw a dark silhouette appear behind the gunner in the turret. The tall, proud bearing suggested it was her friend. Heelee grinned and rushed in. She watched the woman in the turret move, a motion so fast a rattlesnake might be jealous. The gunner's neck snapped. The turret was unmanned.

Standing up on Hop's hindquarters was a feat for a trick rider. Heelee found pleasure practicing moves with Hop when the plains revealed no enemies. She craved the smuggler's big gun and knew Fonn would leave it untouched as a baaschiili weapon. She urged Hop faster, catching up to the noxious stinkwagon. Crouching, she waited for a moment for her eyes to adjust to the black-on-black of her target. She jumped, reaching out for a handhold. Something clacked against the stinkwagon as she landed, and fell. She thought it was her knife but couldn't stop to check. Reaching out, she managed to attain the side of the stinkwagon, but it was slick. Her fingers slid down the side, until she caught the barest weld-edge. It was enough. She found better footing and pushed herself up, catching a grip.

Making her way to the turret took all her concentration. She heard the sounds of combat all around her. By the sounds of it one of her bandmates had made it inside the wagon. She wondered who. Pressing her eye to the slit, she could see several figures. She heard the baby cry before she saw the black bundle in the girl's arms. The girl was as skinny as a coydog, pale and big-eyed and too young to have a child, even an infant such as this one. Next to her was a bear of an old man, too big to make out properly in the dark, save for his silvery beard. He held his weapon as though he had a target in his sights, and Heelee looked down to see one of her bandmates unmoving on the floorboards.

"There's another one, Pa!" The skinny coydog girl pointed with her whole arm, then swiftly grabbed the baby that was no longer secure.

A bullet pinged off the inside of the stinkwagon. "Stay away, strangers, this is my family and I aim to protect 'em."

Heelee wanted to keep heading towards the turret. The gun up top was so big, and she could keep it as a symbol of her prowess, using it against other enemies. To see children with children, it wasn't how smugglers did things. They were men, risking their lives for gold. They knew the risks. These were innocents, and they shouldn't be involved.

The turret called to her, though, and her hands were tiring, and this was a dangerous place. She kept climbing. She heard the cries of her sisters, the cries of triumph. She reached the turret. She looked down to see Challa and Donya prying the back off the cargo space. She looked around for more smugglers to kill, but the stinkwagon seemed low on smugglers. Something wasn't right.

"Where's Prexxi?" Challa shouted up to Heelee.

Heelee knew, but she also knew to say would be the death of the infant and the girl. "I'll go look," she offered instead.

The climb down was no better than the climb up, but this time Heelee found a hatch. She entered quietly, but the gasp of the girl brought the man to aim on her with speed.

"They will kill you, you must leave." Using the tongue of the technological people was difficult, but it was part of her training.

"What about you?" the man asked. He looked down at Prexxi. "Why aren't you killing us?"

"Her. Her." She pointed at the girl and her baby. "Innocent."

"Just like that, huh?" The old man scoffed. "Bullshit."

Whatever Heelee might have said blew away in the detonation that followed. Metal sang and tore. Heelee grabbed the girl and her baby and jumped as far as she could. The concussive force of the blast knocked them out before they hit the ground.

Pain washed over Heelee. She looked down to see her skin, burned black. The girl nearby seemed to be sleeping peacefully. Heelee tried to move to wake her, to relieve her pain as her neck appeared to be at an awkward angle. It was difficult to tell, her vision was strained and blurry. A tiny bundle of furious anger threw his fists in the air. His skin was unbroken and he landed atop his mother, cushioning his fall. Heelee snorted. A boy child. She'd gone to all this trouble for a boy child.

The next time Heelee woke, the pain was less, but her vision still swam. She hadn't noticed the first time, but it was as though proper distance evaded her. She struggled to sit up. Her hands were swathed in bandages, up her arms, and down her leg. She gasped, double checking. She had both hips, both thighs, both knees, but beyond that, only one calf, one ankle, one foot. The stinkwagon had killed her. She reached up to feel for her talisman, and hissed. It wasn't there.

"Your luck has abandoned you." Wind's Melody's voice was recognizable. Heelee turned towards the left, where her vision revealed the winter apple woman. "Or your curse has caught up to you. Or perhaps both."

"What happens now, Elder?" Heelee tried to keep the tremble of fear from her voice.

The sympathetic look from Wind's Melody was enough that tears sprang to her eye. "You are dead, Heelee. You rescued a boy child from a smuggler's stinkwagon instead of avenging the death of your bandmate, Prexxi. Your shame is heaped upon your shame."

"Then why heal me?" Anger flooded her, anger and helplessness. "Why bring me back into this broken vessel if you will not keep me?"

"Death is a release, child." Her voice was steel wrapped in velvet.

"What is to become of me, then, Elder?" Heelee forced the flood of her panic down. "I am dead but not dead, rescued from the tribe but unable to live within it?"

"You know your crimes, now. Perhaps you can find your death in the prairie, and let your body feed the coydogs." Wind's Melody stood up, and turned her back on Heelee. "Baatach xaxua baaluuk."

When she was alone, Heelee wept until she was exhausted. She fell asleep, only to be woken by a child leaving her a plate of food. Heelee didn't want to eat, but she forced herself to. This was no longer a safe place, and she had to leave.

It was an unexpected gift to find a package of travel clothes, a bag of rations, a knife, and water. When she left the tent, she saw that Hop wasn't saddled for her. He was paddocked with Nightdrop and the others. A long, sturdy stick was leaned against the tent near the door. Even with it, Heelee had a slow walk to leave the camp. All of the adults had their backs turned towards her in silence. The children played between the adult's legs, or stood mimicking their elders.

The going was slow, but Heelee's pride demanded that she made it through this. The hardest moment came when she saw Fonn. Their eyes met, just for a moment. The playful light in Fonn's eyes was gone, replaced by a smoldering hatred. There weren't enough words in the world to set it right, so Heelee didn't try.

She didn't have enough rations or water for a long march, and she would not be able to hunt. Her goal was to walk out into the prairie far enough to not disturb the villagers when she passed to the next world.

Determination and a walking stick helped, but it didn't take long for her to be exhausted. Pain lanced up her leg, and her hand was sore from gripping the walking stick. She was ready to give up when she smelled something.

Cordite.

Curiosity and a burning sense of shame cajoled her towards the defeated stinkwagon. A pyre burned here, to honor the dead. Apsaalooka burned their enemies, to prevent anyone from winning back their dead. Another site nearby, the ground lay open like a raw wound. Twisted metal peppered the area. Heelee found a bullet on the ground, and another one nearby. Different calibers, different casings, and neither of them fired. How strange.

She found an enormous black pistol, somehow undamaged, lying in the bent and broken grass. A Zerorez. It was too big to be practical for her, but she put it in her pack for possible trade later. Discovering that she wasn't resigned was a suprise to her.

Heelee made a fire amidst the wreckage. It wasn't the carefully constructed fire pit of her Chiaxxa Bia ways, but instead the tired flailings of an invalid. She didn't care who saw the smoke. She didn't care if it drove prey away. She was going to stay here, where she should have died, until she did.

"That's a bit sloppy of you, isn't it?" A deep, growling voice like a bear given words came from behind her. "It leaves you open to attack."

She turned to see a big man, swathed in black, from his wide-brimmed hat to his shiny boots. He had a silvery beard that she recognized. His gun was leveled on her, a rifle. He looked her up and down, appraising her as though he was looking to buy a horse.

"You lived." She observed.

"As did you." He looked at her again. "Well, mostly."

She shook her head. "I am dead."

"Obviously. My mistake." He took a step closer to her. She flinched, but did not move. "You saved Jeremiah."

"He's with my people." Heelee said. "They won't give him back."

The man shrugged. "He'll have a better life there anyway."

"Are you going to kill me?" She asked hopefully.

"That seems like bad form, considering you saved my grandchild. It looks like you can't stay here though. Is that because you saved him?" he asked.

"Our ways are not your ways. It is hard to explain." She watched him take another step nearer. He lowered his rifle.

"Do you really want to die, NaN girl?" he asked gruffly.

"Today I do. Tomorrow...I will."

"You might be dead to your people, but that doesn't mean you have to die. Come with me. I'm on my way to Seattle. We can get you a new leg and maybe do something about your eye." The old man stuck out his hand. "My name is Simon, by the way."

She paused.

"You lost your name, too, didn't you?" Simon shook his head. "I know some about your people. Let's give you a name. I'll call you Ganada. My poor wife doesn't need that name anymore."

Named after a dead woman. She found it to be appropriate. Ganada accepted her name. "I will travel with you, at least for a ways, Simon. I wish to know more about this leg and eye."

"Well, it's a few days' travel, what with your injuries. There's a smugglers' camp not far from here, where we can get supplies and maybe catch the next caravan." He looked at his hand, and then at her.

She grasped his hand, allowed him to pull her up. "If I do not find Seattle to my liking, I will kill you."

"You and what army? C'mon, Ganada, maybe you can help save a few more lives before you're taken out." Simon held out a rock with a leather thong through it. "Is this yours? It looks like something your people'd wear."

Ganada gasped and reached out before pulling her hand away. "It is mine."

Simon smiled. "Well, let's get this back on you and get on our way."

"It is a sign. I will go with you, Simon." She looked out towards the grasslands, slightly dizzy from her damaged vision. "Lead the way."

THE RELUCTANT AUTHOR

MEGAN J. PATTON

Megan has two writing degrees that do not pay the bills. She got her BFA from Hartwick College in 2008. After graduation Megan had a soul crushing career in the fast paced and flashy world of corporate pharmaceutical insurance validation. She obtained her MA from Wilkes University in 2010, and thankfully gave up her career as a vitamin D deficient cubicle monkey. Megan is working on a dystopian series, and is the author of The Magical Time Keeper serial currently published with Jukepop Serials. She also does manuscript review for friends and spends too much time looking at cat pictures on the internet.

Alma died in her tidy New York home shortly after 5pm on October 17th, before the news came on but after the daytime talk shows ended. No one noticed that they were short one Alma Perch, aged sixty-five, quiet librarian and widow of Melvin Perch, a mild-mannered ornithologist who discovered a rare type of pigeon in the late eighties. This discovery brought him mild academic fame but nobody was really that impressed: this impacted nothing, and the general consensus was that the Perch Pigeon was going to shit on your car no matter what. Still, the Perch family was well liked and the neighbors mourned Alma once they realized she'd left them.

The coroner said he'd never seen anything like it and refused to talk about the Perch case to anyone after the investigation was over. After signing her death certificate, he offered his resignation and moved to Connecticut to open a rare book shop. The funeral director in charge of Alma's remains took an early retirement soon after her funeral. His bewildered sons sold the business and reported that their father was sailing around the world in a cruiser with sails that snapped happily in the wind. Alma's death was recorded as natural and listed as heart failure. Everyone involved agreed that the body be cremated. It was just too weird.

She was found on November 4th by a trustee of the library who was concerned when Alma didn't show up for two weeks and didn't answer her phone. There was no bloated corpse lying in sweet repose, squishily leaking into the arm chair, no malodorous stench clinging to the curtains and the carpet. Alma sat with her hands in her lap and her head leaning back, resting lightly on the upholstery. She was cold—her skin a creamy white under all the blue—and papery dry. Rigor mortis had come and gone and despite the anomalies, she looked quite alive. The trustee, Bertie St. Louis, gingerly reached out to touch Alma's neat hair, knowing full well the old girl was gone. The house had that air about it; it ached with the stillness that comes to a room when there are no heartbeats reverberating across the walls. Alma's head lulled to the side with a quiet rustle and Bertie began to scream—long, high-pitched and theatrical. For years afterward, Bertie recounted the story of Finding Alma Perch to her new friends in Atlantic City over neon-colored cocktails as the old girls cooed and clucked what-a-shame, tutting and ruffling their feathers as they exchanged other gruesome Help-I've-Fallen unfound moments: broken hips in the bathtub, toast smoldering in the kitchen while the air thickens around a small frail shape, fetal on the linoleum. It wasn't like that for Alma. Bertie never bothered to explain that part, and just smiled sadly with a nod and a sip of her luridly colored drink and felt very much alive. Funny how death does that to a person.

John Schwartz, having lived a few houses down from Alma, was the first to respond to Bertie's cries of shock and horror. A veteran of the police force for thirty years, John thought he'd seen everything. A year later, he would tell his new girlfriend (a pretty, tanned divorcée who he'd meet on "the computer") all about the Alma Perch case, how her eyes still followed him sometimes, button-black and brimming with the unknowable. This story would earn him a busty, perfumed hug, and probably something more.

Foul play had been everyone's first impression—they couldn't figure that she would have done that to herself. After the investigation yielded no answers and the autopsy went down in morgue lore as "creepy as fuck", the book was closed on poor Alma.

Alma's heart was blackened and enlarged. There were abrasions in the tissue, fine and delicate, as if someone had scraped a needle over her heart—pinpricks and dashes and long jagged scrapes. Words. All of them looping one over the other. The doctor couldn't explain how capillaries on her face had risen to the surface, delicate and spidery, working in intricate patterns across Alma's fine creamy skin, epitaphs and sonnets written—each vein curling into a letter or ending a word.

The more they investigated, the more uneasy they all became for reasons that were too big to understand or explain but still hovered in the periphery of their lives until they gave up searching. It loomed, this giant thing: solid and undefinable in its presence but still frightening. Her bones were engraved, quick pen strokes over white silken tissues, they rippled with words. On her femurs were epics, with script flowing like ivy vines. Her clavicles, haikus of sunsets and leaves on the wind. On her ribs were poems of love and hate, of despair, triumph and regret. Her tiny stapes bone held only one small inscription, like a warning: listen. At the time of this discovery, a young medical student named Marcus who had been given the task of cataloguing Alma's malady could almost hear her whisper it at the edge of his hearing, a little flicker of sound. There was no blood in her veins, but a deep blue-black tarry substance. A coldness crept up his neck and there were blotches of ink staining his lab coat, Rorschach-spattered and dark. He left her there—cracked open on the cold table, words and heart and brain exposed to the world—and walked away. That hovering feeling, that looming, lessened with each squeak of his wingtips on the tile floor. Prayers and hosannas were drafted across her palms and journeys dictated on the soles of her feet—Marcus recited them to himself as he walked quickly towards the exit. He loosened his tie and kept walking, feet planted firmly west, where the mountains were, in the direction of the first one he would climb, swinging freely hand hold to foot hold, the sun on his back and his face to the stone.

Her teeth were the worst. Alma's teeth had been smashed in, broken into jagged little barbs, and sharp splinters of them were found sprinkled down her neck and chest, coated with the same blue-black ink. The police wanted to believe that someone cracked her in the face with an inkwell. The coroner was determined to say it was drug related because he wasn't a very creative man and the idea of drugs frightened him, as did Alma's case, so he put two and two together just because they shared a common fear. Straws, of course. Something small and insignificant to grasp at. What they were ignoring, what they pretended none of them saw, was that her tongue had shrunk and sharpened to a point like a quill and was tipped black.

A forensic dentist they called in to look at Alma's teeth promptly returned all the evidence including the molds, x-rays, and specimens, quit her job and moved to the mountains with her husband and young daughter to open up a ski lodge. When approached by a curious medical student several months later, the dentist wouldn't speak to him but gave the phone to her three-year-old daughter who tortured the agonized student with her musings on children's television programming and potty training until the demoralized young man hung up. He did not call again.

One thing the dentist never told anyone, not even her husband, was that she kept one of Alma Perch's bicuspids: the smooth white enamel etched in as if with a laser, so small and fine the writing that it was almost invisible to the naked eye. But, after many impressions and enlargements and photographs it was all there just the same—a fragment of a sentence, just a half formed idea that struck her in a way she never understood. She kept the tooth in the bottom of her sock drawer in an old box that her business checks came in.

Nobody ever knew. Her life unspooled before her in a happy and winding trail of seasonal ski rentals, late check-ins, her husband's flushed cheeks after a cold day on the mountain, and her daughter's sleeping form, one hand curled on a pink fluffy blanket and one wrapped around a stuffed moose.

Coronary artery disease was ruled out after Alma's heart dried up. It crumbled away to a greasy pile of ashes when the coroner poked at it with tweezers. It was impossible to get a blood sample as all of the tarry ink had clogged in the tubing and hardened into sticky clots. The medical tools used to crack Alma's sternum, to cut open her cranium, to drain the blood from her veins were blocked with the substance. It was decided the tools should be thrown out. Jessie, an intern with ghoulish curiosity, pocketed the hagedorn needle used to sew the skin back together over Alma's ribs—one flap over the other like an envelope—and showed it to her friends one night when they were all young and vibrant and full of the possibilities of their innocence. All those involved that night passed the needle from one to the other, shaking it side to side in the plastic tube with frightened glee. One bold youth exclaimed he was going to open the container and examine the needle more closely. He did this with the hope of impressing Jessie. There were girlish squeaks of horrified delight and brave macho chuffing in amused disbelief. The young man popped the top off and slid the needle out into the palm of his hand. It rested there: innocuous and dull. A nervous titter bubbled up from Jessie's throat and she felt uneasy in a wordless way. That needle was wrong, cursed maybe, infected, and she should have thrown it out with the other instruments. Panicked, she slapped the needle out of his hand only to pierce her own skin. Her friends watched, eyes alight with gruesome fascination as she plucked the needle from her finger tip. Would she fall asleep for a thousand years? Would her hand turn black and rot off? Would she begin foaming at the mouth and attack a nearby bar patron? They all tensed, readying to jump if they had to catch her, run from her, subdue her. She blinked for a moment and let the incredible itching sensation pass over her. Everything felt wrong. Her own skin didn't fit. She did not belong at that bar, with those people, in that time or that place. Smiling, she slung her purse over her shoulder and waved a distracted goodbye. The young man who had held the needle looked stunned, she patted his shoulder absently as she walked past. Jessie didn't feel the same way about him and didn't want to lead him on. She twirled her car keys around her punctured finger tip and wondered if she could really make it as a painter. Years later, her haunting works centered around portraits of a dead woman would be selling for astronomical amounts and the art gallery patrons would be horrified and fixated by the delicate, haunting face of Alma Perch, immortalized forever in oils.

***

All of this information: the odd biological findings, the high emotions, the fear, was kept quiet when Bertie called Auggie Perch and told him his mother had died. If they had told Auggie about how they found her, they would have had answers to the frightening yet curious circumstances of Alma's death. The town was half convinced there was a tattoo artist serial killer hunting their tidy suburban streets, ready to attack and mutilate with the deft whirrrrrrr of his tattoo gun. All Auggie had been told of his mother's death was that they were pretty sure it was heart failure, but they couldn't rule out foul play, but they didn't have a suspect, and they'd accidentally cremated her.

On a rainy November afternoon Auggie Perch found himself outside his childhood home, his mother's ashes in his hands and the cool ceramic of the urn warming by the heat of his palms. Inside the house he knew his father's field work was still stacked neatly on the desk in his study, the prints from the Audubon Society still hung on the blue and white flowered wallpaper, the remote still rested on the coffee table between a dish of mints and the TV guide.

He fumbled for his keys and opened the door; cold rain dripped from the eaves down the back of his collar. He put Alma's urn down gently on the kitchen counter and flicked on the hall light to begin the merciless hunt for her will.

Augie searched for the better part of the afternoon, but he found little more than the usual crumbs of a life: ticket stubs, dry cleaning receipts, match books, dusty buttons, mismatched earrings.

Augie had few regrets in a life that was spotless and smooth like a clear pane of glass. His parents were loving and good people; he was educated and good with money, so he took the next logical step and became a banker—making money not only for himself but many other people as well. It took him a very long time to realize his days felt like an empty and constant plod to nowhere. He knew he was alive in the way all of us know we're alive: because people still expected him to do things. Nobody asks you for favors or expects you to do anything if you're dead.

Sitting in his mother's closet, these thoughts battered him, flapping their dark and slippery wings around his face. He moved clothes, packed boxes. Under the Christmas decorations was a small chest full of blank journals and notebooks. Their empty pages fluttered restlessly as he picked up the first one: red leather bound with a gold silk ribbon marking the first page. The inscription read:

> *"To Alma,*
> *Love Mother.*
> *December, 1976."*

The next one read the same save for the date and the others under it as well, some from his father, or aunt, or a library patron, the pages glowing with possibility and hope locked away in a gleaming trunk under a dusty blanket. He remembered then, with a clarity that hurt, the first time he realized he could write a sentence that would be read by other people. He was young, and very small for his age, sitting at the kitchen table with a yellow pencil clutched in his little fist and his toes swinging above the floor. He looked at the paper in front of him, at his craggy hesitant pencil strokes and mouthed the words he had written over and over again. Auggie looked at the small sentence; it was little like he was, and so unprotected in the world of words. He wanted to shield it from everyone, take it somewhere far away and plant it so the words could grow bigger. Alma had noticed him struggling and watched him sharply over the kitchen counter. She stirred a pot with no heed to the sauce slopping over the sides. Auggie thought long and hard about how vulnerable his words were and angrily tore the page out of his workbook and threw them into the trash. He thought he could hear the letters rattle at the bottom of the can as they slipped off the page. He put his head down on the table and cried. It wasn't a skinned-knee, little boy cry, these were the tears of someone learning a lesson far too harsh at too young an age. Alma sighed and stopped stirring. She squatted down next to Auggie and nuzzled his shoulder.

"Mamma," he said between sharp little sobs, "Mamma, there's words in my heart but I don't know how to let them out."

"You'll learn how, Auggie," she said, stroking the wispy curls at the nape of his neck. "You'll learn, baby."

"But what if I don't? What if I can't?" he wailed, burying his face in her shoulder. She sighed and rocked him, saying nothing.

That memory folded over him like a blanket and suddenly the rumors all made sense. Unlike the rest of the town, Auggie had known his mother's way with words. He could see the gentle but firm way her hand held a book, reverently and with awe. He also could have told them how white her face would become when forced to confront the blank page and a pen. Shopping lists terrified her. School excuses were petrifying. It fell to Melvin, in his blocky scientist scribble, to excuse Auggie from class or allow him to go on a field trip. A letter to the electric company was a windmill Alma Perch could not conquer.

Auggie always knew by the look in his mother's eyes and the set of her jaw that there were worlds trapped inside her, struggling to get out: whole eternities that could not be spun out like celestial thread to hang the stars upon. No one understood, least of all Alma, that the words could not stay trapped forever and that it was a cleaner fate to let them out—stampeding out of the pen—than to keep and guard them. The words, they breed, become stories, lives, sunsets, universes.

No one could ever know the storm of them as they boiled under Alma's heart when she couldn't capture the sibilant hiss of the wind through new spring leaves or the gripping cold fear of the empty page. Alma never thought the story would write itself whether she wanted it to or not. A child coming into this world does not mean to bring death to its mother but birth must happen. So it was with Alma's stories, forcing their way out, bursting into the world.

Some years later, after Alma's house had been packed and sold, Auggie hiked to the summit of the nearest mountain and looked at the sweet green view of the valley. His hometown spread beneath him like an unfurled map. The library where Alma worked was tucked into the folds of the land like a bookmark in the middle of some grand novel. Auggie tipped the urn holding his mother's ashes over the edge of the cliff. It did not surprise him when thousands of tiny pieces of paper flew out, soaked with ink and unreadable.

THANK YOU

Many thanks to our patrons
and supporters, especially:

KE JAECK
TORY HOKE
JESSICA POWELL

Want to see your name here? Become a patron!
patreon.com/lunastation

ABOUT THE COVER

OCTAVIA BUTLER

Pioneering and talented writer, Octavia Butler can best be summed up in her own words:

"Who am I? I am a forty-seven-year-old writer who can remember being a ten-year-old writer and who expects someday to be an eighty-year-old writer. I am also comfortably asocial—a hermit.... A pessimist if I'm not careful, a feminist, a Black, a former Baptist, an oil-and-water combination of ambition, laziness, insecurity, certainty, and drive."

These characteristics threaded their way into her writing, helping her win awards, and becoming the first science fiction writer to win the MacArthur Foundation Fellowship.

ERIN DEMOSS

Erin is a graphic designer from Oklahoma who geeks out over typography and information design. She has been interested in art all her life and fell in love with graphic design and illustration while going to school for public relations. She is a cat lady, a Leo, and a Star Wars nut. Her favorite book is American Gods by Neil Gaiman and her spirit animal is Louise Belcher.

You can find more of her work at erindemoss.com

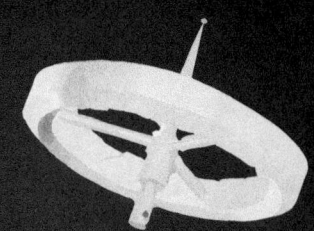